TWO MASKS
ONE HEART III

Boss Lady

A Novel

JACOB SPEARS

TRAYVON JACKSON

Good 2 Go Publishing

TWO MASKS ONE HEART III

Written by Jacob Spears and Trayvon Jackson
Cover design: Davida Baldwin
Typesetter: Mychea
ISBN: 9781943686520

Copyright ©2016 Good2Go Publishing
Published 2016 by Good2Go Publishing
7311 W. Glass Lane • Laveen, AZ 85339
www.good2gopublishing.com
https://twitter.com/good2gobooks
G2G@good2gopublishing.com
www.facebook.com/good2gopublishing
www.instagram.com/good2gopublishing

We would like to truly dedicate this book to our forever beloved brother, Eriese Tisdale. And to Charmaine Tisdale, woman, keep strong! And to every mother who has a son on death row, just know that the system is not God and prayers are genuinely the key to life. As well, we would like to dedicate this book to Shannon Eighmie and Julie Scott.

~ Jacob Spears and Trayvon Jackson

From both of us, we would like to congratulate Sergeant Polite and give a shout out to Deputy Tolley and to our fans. Enjoy and continue to rock!

~ Jacob Spears and Trayvon Jackson

Acknowledgements

I send my sincere love to my family, starting with my beloved mother, Lenora Sarantos. I love you, Mom! To my sisters, Amy McKinney, Tabatha Hopkins, and Heather Hopkins, I love you three unconditionally—never doubt that. I would like to shout out to my cousin, Eleah Huff. Keep succeeding, cuzo! And finally, and with all due respect, I would like to give a fat-ass shout out to Mychea! Continue to push that pen.

~ Jacob Spears

I would like to thank Good2Go once again for making this book and to work diligently with a true friend and succeed, possible. I give a shout out to my entire family including my mother, Frankie Mae Jackson; woman, you are the woman of my dreams. To all my siblings, big brother is coming home—it's just a time thing. A shout out to Travon Jamison; we bear almost the same name. Keep your head up, brah. Another shout out to Chico Miguel Maldonado. You always looking out. To my nigga, Va, thanks for the paper to keep me supplied. And to Latoya Moye, woman, it's amazing how God placed you in my life to rock with me the way you do, and I appreciate you 100 percent. What's up, Vibe? I told you I was for real. And to the one who knows these numbers best: 1, 4, 3 . . .

~ Trayvon Jackson

Wisdom

What we see with our eyes could be deceiving. It could affect the heart by misleading. Control your mind and guard your heart, because sometimes what's dark is really the light, like love that can't be explained—ineffable.

~ *Trayvon Jackson*

TWO MASKS
ONE HEART III

Boss Lady

One

"So, this is how you're gonna play, huh?" Jarvis spoke out loud in the confines of his home, highly inebriated from the excessive use of alcohol. "Where are you, motherfuc-kers?" he said sluggishly before he downed the last of his Hennessy, slamming down the glass on the counter of his mini bar.

It had been two weeks since Champagne's abduction, and he was still waiting for Tameka to call him back. Jarvis was torn apart and mentally devastated. Big Dee's murder was all over Jonesboro, and the club was closed due to an ongoing investigation by the city. Jarvis was tired of the authorities constantly harassing him and trying to question him about Big Dee's death.

Shit! I am in as much suspense as them motherfuckers! Jarvis thought as he poured himself another drink of straight Hennessy.

He was alone and afraid for Champagne's life. Shaquana was constantly calling her phone, but Jarvis would never answer. It was a good thing that she had no clue where Jarvis's mansion was located in Bankhead, or else Shaquana would have come over to check up on her friend.

"Come on, bitch! Call me!" Jarvis screamed out in rage while throwing the glass against the concrete wall behind the bar, smashing it to pieces.

Jarvis broke down into hysterics for the umpteenth time since Tameka had taken his woman.

"I'ma kill that bitch!" he yelled out, right as he heard his iPhone ring.

"Hello!" he answered sluggishly.

* * *

"Damn! Somebody is taking it hard. I'd never expected to see you get so mad over a bitch!" Tameka said into her iPhone 6 to Jarvis.

She was using an app to disguise her number. She was enjoying the Miami sun in her red bikini while relaxing in a beach chair and drinking a martini. Next to her was D-Zoe, taking in the nice view of beautiful South Beach, where Tameka had purchased a luxurious beach house and shacked up with D-Zoe, who she had found to be very elegant and kind, and was someone to have around as a sexual partner.

"So, tell me, Jarvis . . . what are we going to do about Ms. Cognac . . . ?"

"Her name isn't Cognac!" Jarvis responded, hearing Tameka and a male laughing in the background on the other end of the phone.

This ho got me on speaker phone, he thought.

"He is funny!" Jarvis heard D-Zoe say.

"Here, baby! Can you fill my glass up . . . and give me a moment, please?" Tameka asked while handing her empty glass to D-Zoe.

"No problem, my princess," he responded as he kissed her on the lips loud enough for Jarvis to hear.

"You have yourself nothing, nigga, whoever the fuck you are!" Jarvis screamed out to D-Zoe.

"Last time I checked, you have yourself nothing, especially after she took the entire football team. She has no feeling to any dick no more!" D-Zoe said, laughing, before he took off to go refill Tameka's glass.

Tameka laughed to herself and stared at D-Zoe's model-like body that was covered in tattoos, as he strutted inside the beach house. Jarvis was going bananas on the phone, in a raging fit.

"Bitch! You raping her? I will fucking kill you and your pussy-ass Jamaicans. You hear me . . . ?"

"Jarvis, please settle down, and let's talk about Ms. Cognac . . ."

"Her name is 'Pagne, Meka, okay!" Jarvis said.

"Whatever, nigga! Her ass is worn out, and she probably don't know her own name anymore. But enough! Let's talk!" Tameka began.

"You want her . . . then let's talk money . . ."

"How much, Tameka, huh?" Jarvis quickly retorted, for money was nothing to him.

"I want you to pay for all the pain you've caused me . . ."

"What are you talking about, Meka?" he asked, perplexed.

"Jarvis, you robbed me out of a good man and chose to step into his shoes. Then you tricked me and had me thinking that we could have gone somewhere . . ."

Bitch, we never had a chance. You cutthroat whore! Jarvis thought.

"I really cared about you. I never had no one to put their hands on me," Tameka said, holding back a storm of tears as she dealt with a surge of emotions.

Jarvis could sense her rush of emotions despite being highly inebriated, and he hated himself at the moment for not taking her seriously.

But she was no better for me than a dead man. She cutthroated Benjamin. What the . . . ! he thought.

"Tameka . . . be real with yourself. What have you done to actually convince me that I could've trusted you?" Jarvis asked as he walked behind the counter of his bar to retrieve another glass.

"I've been faithful to you and trusted your heart. But honestly, you're so concerned about a person's past." She paused for a second. "Jarvis, you're no different than my ex. Why didn't I cut your throat when you were asleep?" Tameka said, surprising him.

Damn! he thought.

"Did it ever come 'cross your mind?" Jarvis asked as he poured himself more Hennessy before taking a long sip.

"Never! But now I wish that I would've seen your betrayal, because I would reconsider."

"Oh, so you did think about it? What was the word again—reconsider? To reconsider means to reflect back on something that you're contemplating or have . . ."

"Let's stop the bullshit, Jarvis. This is no longer about us. You have . . . well . . . you're worried 'bout saving this bitch of yours. So let's talk about her, okay?" Tameka said as D-Zoe emerged from the beach house with her martini.

"Where is she, Tameka?" Jarvis begged sadly.

"She's somewhere safe until you break the rules, Jarvis."

"Listen! What are you asking for?" Jarvis wanted to know.

"I need half a billion, Jarvis!"

"Million?" Jarvis checked for assurance.

"Billion!" Tameka responded.

"Bitch! Is you crazy? I don't have that type of money!" Jarvis exploded.

Click!

Before Jarvis could finish his raging fit, Tameka hung up on him and then grabbed the glass from D-Zoe.

"Thank you, baby," Tameka said, kissing him on his lips.

"You're welcome always, princess!" D-Zoe retorted, joining her back on a chair on the beach.

"Your friend has no respect for a real woman. Let me handle him," D-Zoe said, almost blinding Tameka with his shining golds.

"Damn, nigga! Remind me to wear shades next time . . . and he's not my friend. This is my friend," Tameka said while rubbing her hands on D-Zoe's adorable model chest and then down to his bulging manhood.

"So, this is your friend, huh?" D-Zoe said while he stood up and pulled out his enormous, throbbing dick.

Tameka quickly wrapped her hands around his erect love tool and placed him inside her mouth while holding her martini in her left hand.

"Yes, baby gal!" D-Zoe purred out to the sweet slow fellation that she was giving him.

I love this dick, but I will not let it control me, nor will I let it love me, she thought as she sucked his cock.

She was done trying to get a man to love her, and she had given up on relationships.

Like business, it is nothing personal; fuck me good and expect for nothing to go past fuck friends, Tameka thought as she felt D-Zoe about to come to his load.

She then intensified her deep-throating and allowed him to release in her mouth.

* * *

"Damn it!" Jarvis yelled when he heard the call disconnect.

He had no clue when Tameka would call him back, and he had no way to contact her. He hated how she had him torn apart, and he badly wanted to know where Champagne was being held.

"Half a billion dollars! That bitch is crazy!" Jarvis exclaimed. "Where the fuck am I going to get that kind of money?"

Jarvis went to pour himself another glass of cognac, but noticed the bottle was empty.

Damn! he thought as he wobbled to the living room and collapsed on the leather sofa.

"I can't believe this shit!" Jarvis said as he rubbed his eyes from fatigue and extreme drunkenness.

When he thought about Champagne, he asked himself if she was worth the risk. As he continued to think about her smile and genuine love, Jarvis knew that the tables had indeed turned against him from when he tested Benjamin's love for her.

"He died for her . . . and I would die about mine," he said.

Jarvis then mumbled to himself before dozing off to sleep.

It wasn't long before he saw Champagne. She was smiling at him as she ran up with her arms spread open. Her hair was soaking wet, and her black bikini was damp.

"Champagne," he mumbled in his sleep.

As she came closer, a woman appeared from out of nowhere behind her. His heart started to race when he saw the woman raise a gun toward Champagne's back. He recognized the woman as Tameka. When he tried to move, he was unable to, and when he tried to speak, he was voiceless. He couldn't call out to Champagne or warn her.

"Die, bitch!" he heard Tameka say as she pulled the trigger.

Boom!

"Nooo!" Jarvis screamed as he came out of his sleep sweating excessively, with his heart pounding rapidly in his chest.

"It's just a dream!" he told himself before he dozed off again.

Two

Maurice awoke to the smell of fried eggs, bacon, and grits, along with a throbbing headache from a hangover from the night before.

It was Arab Hajji's going-away party, and the 12th Street niggas celebrated through the early morning hours.

Damn! That shit was extra swole, Maurice thought as he rolled from bed and strutted to the bathroom. He brought Shaquana with him and saw the envious-ass bitches trying to strip her title away with their envious stares.

Them hoes were hot as hell seeing that bad bitch on my arms, he thought as he reached into the medicine cabinet and grabbed a bottle of Advil. He quickly grabbed a pill and washed it down with a gulp of water from the sink.

As he brushed his teeth, the smell of breakfast intensified. He was grateful to have a woman with queenly traits.

These days, a man has to remind a woman how to be a woman . . . but not all of them are self-centered, he thought.

Damn, I have to go holla at C-Murder today, Maurice reminded himself.

After Maurice hopped out of the shower and put on a pair of Jordan shorts and a matching black wifebeater, he went to find Shaquana. She was still in the kitchen, bent over and checking on a pan of buttered biscuits in the oven. She was dressed in a mini house dress and wore no panties underneath. Maurice caught a splendid view of her curvaceous buttocks running away from her dress.

"Damn, baby! You know that's against the law," Maurice said as he walked up on her.

"Oh, really! Says who?" Shaquana answered as she shut the oven door and wrapped her arms around Maurice's neck, bringing him down to her and kissing him.

The taste of Colgate toothpaste was fresh on his breath, and she savored every taste of his mouth, trying to push her tongue to the back of his throat. When she pulled back for a moment to breathe, she pecked him on his lips and looked into his eyes.

"Good morning, my king!" she said.

"Is it a good morning or about to be a good morning, once I get to eating," Maurice retorted while grabbing a handful of Shaquana's ass and shaking it.

"Baby! I hope you're talking about this delicious breakfast that I've slaved to make for you . . . and not what you've been eating all night," Shaquana said, referring to their great sexual foreplay the previous night.

"Damn, baby! I still want some of that too!"

"I know, but there's not enough time, baby. I have to go to a meeting to register for school, remember?" she told him while preparing him a hefty plate.

"Damn! My bad! It must be this hangover," Maurice considered.

"Here! Hold this!" Shaquana asked as she shoved the plate into Maurice's hands while she opened up the oven to retrieve two hot biscuits with her bare hands.

"Shit!" she yelled out, quickly placing the biscuits on his plate and then fanning her hands, in an attempt to cool them down.

9

"Try to wear oven mitts. They're right there!" he said, looking at them sitting on the counter.

"Boy! It's a sista trait to burn her hands in the kitchen. That means a bitch putting her foot down, baby. Now come . . . let's sit down and stuff our faces," Shaquana said as she escorted Maurice to the table and pulled out his seat for him to sit down.

"Damn, baby! I really appreciate this. I can't recall if a woman has ever pulled out a chair for me."

"Well, there's a first time for everything," Shaquana said.

After she fixed herself a plate of food, Shaquana joined Maurice at the table with two glasses of 100 percent orange juice. Together they ate their breakfast and fed each other from time to time.

When Shaquana began to struggle to finish the food on her plate, Maurice grabbed her plate and ate the rest.

"Damn, nigga! You so greedy!" Shaquana joked.

"And I can still consume plenty of dessert," Maurice retorted, licking his lips and then seductively flicking his tongue at her like he did when he was making love to her clitoris.

Shaquana got the picture, and despite her getting moist between her legs, she couldn't. Today was an important day, and she couldn't be late.

"No, Maurice! Get it out of your head!" Shaquana said as she grabbed their empty plates and carried them over to the sink.

"I'll handle that, baby. Go get yourself ready, okay?" Maurice suggested as he took over.

"Okay. Ummm, thanks!" Shaquana said as she strutted away.

As she left, Maurice watched her undulations and the way her ass jiggled at her every step. It made him grateful for the beautiful woman who was all his.

In the steaming shower, Shaquana became stressed—like she had so often lately—when thinking about Champagne. She had no clue why Champagne wasn't picking up her phone, and she had no idea where she and Jarvis lived.

Maybe I ran her off with that school mess. If I did, I still didn't force nothing on her, Shaquana thought as she rinsed the soap off her body and then stepped out to dry off.

"Baby, I'm gone!" she heard Maurice yell out to her.

"So you're just going to leave like that?" she called to him.

"I didn't say I'm out of here . . ."

"Whatever, nigga! Don't even try that shit. You were gone," Shaquana said as she dried her body and Maurice stood in the doorway.

As she dried off her inner thighs, Maurice couldn't help his erection that betrayed him as he watched her shaven plump pussy wink at him.

Damn! he thought as he walked up and embraced her.

"Do you love me?" he asked.

"Damn! What kind of question is that, Maurice?" she said as she looked into his eyes.

"A question that demands an answer."

"Yes, I love you, Maurice . . . and I mean every word of it."

"I know you do. I just like hearing you profess to me sometimes . . ."

"I tell you every time . . . like every night, baby," she answered.

11

She then stood on the top of her toes and leaned in to kiss him. Their lips locked, and Maurice kissed her strongly and passionately, causing her to let out a soft moan. She wanted him to take her right there in the bathroom, but she had to run and so did he.

Damn! she thought as she broke away from his addiction and escaped his love spell by running from the bathroom.

"I love you, baby, but I have to go. Can't be late!" she yelled as she hastily dressed herself.

"I love you, baby, and I'll see you later."

"I love you, too. Be safe!" Shaquana added.

She knew that Maurice would be safe and that he could hold his own, but she also knew well that danger had no fear of who it chose to take—like death. Her father had been a well-respected man and had put fear into a lot of niggas' hearts, and he still died in the streets. After seeing how Arab Hajji was killed, Shaquana was afraid for Maurice.

Despite knowing that Arab Hajji caused himself to be killed by the police after chasing a man into Walmart, she tried imagining the things that would make a man lose his mind like Hajji. For the first time, she understood a factor in life, that you never know what the next day will bring or the next moment. She was experiencing that factor in all aspects because she never saw Champagne going mute on her, and she had no clue of the danger she was in.

Three

When Mrs. Gina Brown strutted into the courtroom with her tall, slender, sexy frame, she turned many heads. She was a six three, gorgeous black woman in her mid-thirties, with a dark brown complexion. Everyone watched as she walked over to her client, who was sitting in the jury box. He had praised himself for having the baddest attorney in the courtroom among the females. Tittyboo smiled as she swayed over to him with her long, sexy strides that covered their distant gap in no time.

"Hey there, Thorton. How are they treating you?" she whispered to Tittyboo while covering her mouth with a clipboard to keep their limited privacy among themselves.

"I'm okay . . . and they're treating me like always—a criminal," he replied while fondling with the belly chain around his waist.

"Great! Because we're not looking for any friends. Ummmm . . . do you know why you are here today?" she asked Tittyboo, who had no damn clue that he was scheduled to be in court today.

"No, I wasn't aware . . ."

"Well, today I'm going to argue a pretrial motion for the state to hand over any possible evidence they might be handing out. It's called a motion to compel, and the reason I'm pushing this issue is to gather the state's plans and hidden evidence against you . . ."

What other evidence do they have other than the gun? he wondered.

"So when will we be going to trial or a deal?" Tittyboo asked.

Mrs. Brown sighed for a moment and then said, "Thorton . . . we're trying to get the state riled up, plus we need to know what they have . . ."

"People . . . this courtroom will be in session in approximately one minute. So please, shut off all cellular devices and be seated," the black bailiff said to the courtroom.

He was a stocky, muscular man in his fifties, who folks called He-Man and sometimes Truck because of his massive arms from weightlifting.

"Let me get settled. We will continue to talk after court is over with, okay?" Mrs. Brown said with a smile on her face.

She then walked over to the defense table where other lawyers camped out and were preparing to argue their cases as well.

Where the fuck is Daquan? It's crazy how I never get to see him, Tittyboo thought.

"Please rise for the Honorable Judge Kenny Stuart of Jonesboro," the bailiff announced as the judge strutted into the room wearing his black robe. He was an old white man in his seventies, with a head of gray hair, which was believed to be from his wits and not his age.

"Please be seated, people!" Judge Stuart said in a deep, resounding voice.

He was a judge that many wrongly underestimated to be a shithead, but he was known for his fairness at handling the law, and famous for his harsh sentencing if found guilty before him.

A side door opened up, and the state attorneys filed into the courtroom together. There were six of them who all gathered at the opposite table from the defense lawyers. Among the state attorneys were four men and two unattractive, heavy-set white women.

"The first to come before me is Michael Cranmer," Judge Stuart announced to the court.

Michael was a stalky, old white man who was in his sixties and stood six five. The other inmates called him Big Country. The bailiff came to the jury box and escorted Big Country over to the podium where his lawyer stood awaiting his arrival. His attorney was an older white man from the public defender's office.

"Good morning, Mr. Cranmer. For the record, please speak up so that the court can hear you, and let's not have the same problems like every other time, sir!" the judge said with emphasis.

"Yes, sir!" Big Country yelled into the microphone like a deaf person, causing the courtroom and the judge to erupt into light laughter.

Bang! Bang! Bang!

The judge rapped his gavel.

"Okay, okay! Enough! Mr. Wells . . . what are we here discussing today?" he said to the state attorney, who was too busy laughing to performing his job.

Wells was a short, nerdy-looking state attorney with a pale complexion and fried brain at knowing the law. Most people couldn't believe that he was an attorney for the state, and those were people who worked with him daily.

"Sir, this is a pretrial motion to have Mr. Cranmer examined for mental health purposes before we move forward with a trial date, sir," Mr. Wells said as he walked up to the judge and handed him a copy of the motion that he was arguing.

Judge Stuart looked over the papers quickly and then immediately signed his decision of whether he'd approve or disapproved the state's request.

"Mr. Cranmer . . . please state your name into the microphone and your date of birth, please."

"My name is Batman. I played in a 1962 rock band in Kentucky, and my birthday is June 27, 1962!" Big Country yelled into the mic, again causing the courtroom to erupt in laughter.

"Okay, let's move on. Mr. Spencer . . . do you have any problem with this motion being presented before me?" Judge Stuart asked Big Country's lawyer, who started to fumble with his papers on the surface of the podium.

"Ummm . . . sir, I have no problem if it's an approved or . . ."

"I'm approving the motion and would order that Mr. Cranmer be examined by an expert psychologist. Um . . . let me better word it . . . a licensed psychologist, to establish his competence to stand trial before me," Judge Stuart said as he then banged his gavel and dismissing Big Country.

Another bailiff entered from a side door and escorted Big Country out of the courtroom. Big Country had the insanity seed stored in everyone's head, making it seem as if he was a madman incapable of knowing wrong from right. But in all actuality, Big Country had more wits than the judge himself.

"Thorton Petway, please come forward, young man," Judge Stuart said to Tittyboo, who was then escorted over to the podium where his gorgeous lawyer was waiting for him.

As he approached her, she smiled bright for him, trying to alleviate his nervousness.

"It's okay," she said lowly as he stood next to her.

"Good morning, sir," the judge said.

"Good morning, Your Honor," Tittyboo replied.

"Can you state you name . . . full name . . . young man, and birth date into the mic loud for the record," the judge requested.

"Thorton Petway . . . and my birth date is March 28, 2000, sir," Tittyboo answered.

"Yeah, son. I see. Very young to be on my docket," the judge said while looking at Tittyboo's criminal record in front of him.

"Okay, state. Mr. Brooks . . . this is a motion by the state. Sorry, I mean the defense to compel evidence in case number 21JCO25."

"Sir, we at the moment are still gathering evidence . . ."

"And we the defense need it," Mrs. Brown said, cutting off the other attorney, who was the prosecutor in Jonesboro with a reputation for high convictions. He was a black man in his late fifties or early sixties, with salt-and-pepper hair, who stood five eight.

"Okay, state. Does Petway have his complete discovery?" the judge asked.

"No, sir. This is a murder case, and we're still in the midst of investigating. So . . . no. We have not released the complete discovery. Being that Statute 380.216 of Georgia's guidelines allows us to keep an ongoing investigation up until trial, it's impossible to release everything. Who knows what will happen tomorrow?" Mr. Brooks explained.

Shit bag! Mrs. Brown thought, unable to refute the fact.

"Defense . . . is there a reason to reveal everything now? Are we moving for a speedy trial where this recommendation would be necessary?" the judge asked.

For a moment, Mrs. Brown remained indecisive before she finally sighed and spoke up.

"No, sir. We're not demanding a speedy trial."

"Well, I've decided . . . and I'm denying this motion on the ground that by Georgia law Statute 380.216, the state has until trial to reveal, unless we're preparing for a speedy trial," the judge explained before he then banged his gavel to dismiss Tittyboo and his attorney.

Bang! Bang! Bang!

"Motion denied!" Judge Stuart announced, final and clear for the record.

* * *

When Tittyboo returned from court, his cellmate, Lamar King, was no longer housed there. All of his property was gone, and all that was left was an empty bunk.

"Damn, where the fuck did 'Mar go?" Tittyboo asked his next-door cellmates, who were two older white men indicted for running a meth lab.

"All we recall is seeing him walk out of the cellblock with all his property . . . and not only him," Henry said, who was the larger and older of the two cellmates. His partner's name was Donald, or Don as he preferred to be called.

"Who else gone?" he asked, looking around for Joshah.

"Your friend, Joshah, packed his things too," Don said.

"Damn! Why they move them?" Tittyboo asked.

"Son . . . your guess is as good as mine. Nobody knows," Henry retorted.

18

Damn! That's crazy! Now who the fuck am I going to talk to and . . . trust? Tittyboo thought.

"Nobody come to my cell. I don't have shit to say to no one!" Tittyboo yelled out as he walked into his cell highly upset.

First the damn judge denies my motion . . . now my two trusted niggas just been abducted, he thought, without the slightest clue of what was going on.

He grabbed his urban novel by Kwan called *Hoodlum* and began to read to clear his mind.

This nigga Daquan still not coming forward to free me, man. How could he just sit over there and say fuck me? Tittyboo reflected, feeling more betrayed by Daquan as the day went by and he still sat in jail.

Nothing made sense to Tittyboo. He had no friends, and he definitely had no one to trust around him. At times, Tittyboo was reprehensible to the point that he had forgotten that he played a major part in his incarceration, despite not being the trigger man. It was he who had given the flaka blunt to Daquan, which made him hallucinate and kill Cindy and T-Zoe. It was something that always would cross his mind, but being highly reprehensible, Tittyboo would quickly dismiss his blame.

Telling Lamar and Joshah the story of how he gave Daquan some flaka was his way of venting the burdensome feeling. And when they would tell him that he did nothing wrong and he couldn't control how anyone would react to a specific drug, he felt better and realized they were telling the truth. In his heart, Tittyboo felt that Daquan's intentions were to kill them both, just like he did.

He shot Cindy and then T-Zoe in cold blood, and he wanted to bring me down with him! Damn! Tittyboo thought while shaking his head introspectively. *I can't let this clown bring me down like this, but what am I supposed to do?*

With Romel and Haitian Beny now off the streets, Maurice and his circle easily took over College Park with their new member, C-Murder. It was evident to everyone that C-Murder had quickly replaced Arab Hajji. Despite there being a few Haitian men still holding Haitian Beny down, Maurice was still able to force his power and get the streets to capitulate to his wrath. When he pulled up to 12th, he saw a crowd of people staring at two niggas brawling in the middle of the street.

"What the fuck these niggas fighting for?" Maurice said as he parked his black Lincoln Navigator and stepped out to watch the fight as well.

He knew both of the under-eighteen niggas, who were both from the 12th Street neighborhood.

"Beat that nigga, Vibe!" a pregnant teenage girl cheered for her cousin, who was getting the best of his opponent named Troy.

When Coy saw Maurice, he and C-Murder walked toward him from the crowd.

"What's up, fam?" Coy said, giving Maurice a dap and a fist-to-fist pound.

"Shit good. What's up with y'all two?" Maurice asked while watching Vibe take Troy to the air and slam him down on his neck.

Ouch! Maurice said to himself, for he felt the pain. The impact vibrated the pavement, and Troy was immediately out cold—unresponsive.

"Man, buddy can't be with us no longer," C-Murder said.

"Pussy nigga. I bet that teach your ass to never try that shit again, shawty!" Vibe said to the unconscious Troy, who was dead, unbeknownst to everyone at the time.

"What they fighting for?" Maurice asked C-Murder and Coy.

"Gambling and Troy running his gangsta slide, so Vibe told him to give him a man-to-man and prove that gangsta . . ."

"Oh my God. He dead!" a girl named Tangy screamed, who ran over to Troy's aid to remove him from the street.

"He's not breathing. Someone call the police, please!" she screamed to everyone, who all began to leave the scene to remove themselves from being witnesses.

"Girl, get out of here. If he dead, they going to think you did it!" an old man wisely advised Tangy.

"I can't just leave him out here!" she screamed at the old man.

"Yo, this bitch is tripping!" Coy said to Maurice and C-Murder.

"Hey, C-Murder," Maurice shouted.

"Yeah!"

"Get that bitch from around here, and then meet us back at the trap in Bankhead," Maurice commanded.

"I got ya, shawty," C-Murder answered before he stormed off as the night fell in College Park.

When Maurice and Coy looked over toward Tangy, she was slouched over Troy's lifeless body and crying hysterically.

"Let's get out of here!" Maurice said to Coy as they began to walk back to his SUV. The moment they made it to the Navigator, Maurice and Coy heard a woman cry out.

"Somebody just shot her!"

Together they turned around and saw Tangy slumped on top of Troy's lifeless body. No one heard the Silencer P89 shots from a hidden nearby location. They only saw the results and scrambled for their own safety. C-Murder had hit again.

* * *

When Vibe heard the news about Troy's and Tangy's deaths, he hurried and packed some clothes and other necessities inside a black duffel bag. In no time, he had made it to the Greyhound bus station in College Park and hopped on a bus going south to Florida, where he would lay low at his father's place in Stuart in Martin County.

Shit was crazy! How could one fight lead to a bitch dying? Vibe contemplated as he boarded the Greyhound.

What really had him worried was that someone had shot Tangy in the back of her head twice.

Who the fuck would want to kill Tangy? Vibe thought as he stared out the massive window and then relaxed back into his comfortable seat.

Sitting across from him on the bus was a pretty blonde woman with two little kids with her. She seemed to be checking out Vibe.

"How are you doing tonight, lovely?" Vibe asked the woman. He was both unabashed and frank with his approach.

"I'm okay. My name is April. Where are you heading to?" she asked Vibe, who took a moment to answer her.

For his own sake, he tried to be as meticulous as possible, but he felt that the woman posed no harm.

"Florida . . . and they call me Vibe. You know, like can me and you vibe," he retorted, causing her to laugh and reveal a beautiful Colgate smile.

Damn! She's beautiful, he thought.

"You're funny, Vibe. It's my luck I guess because me and my two boys are on our way to Florida as well."

"Really, where?" Vibe asked ecstatically.

"A couple hours away . . . Tallahassee."

Damn! I just missed her, Vibe thought as he looked at her two well-behaved boys.

"You're taking them to their father or family?" he asked.

"I'm not with their father, and I'm taking them away from him . . . nowhere near him!" she informed Vibe.

Damn! Vibe thought.

"So that means that you're single, huh?"

She was a gorgeous Megan Fox look-alike with blonde hair and exotic green eyes. He gave her a ten for her Coke-bottle frame, which turned him on more.

A white bitch with a body! Vibe said to himself under his breath.

"Yes, I'm single," April told him with a smile.

* * *

A couple hours later, Vibe was giving April an exhaustive round of hard-core sex at her $1.5 million home in a wealthy neighborhood called The Manors.

"Damn it, Vibe! Harder!" she purred as he rapidly thrust inside her sultry mound from behind.

This bitch can take some dick! Vibe thought as he did as she requested and pounded her pink pussy like some type of punching bag, which intensified her moans.

"Yes! Yes!" she yelled out.

While on the bus ride, Vibe decided to change his plans of going to his dad's, especially when she told him that she owned her own home. And the only reason she decided to travel by bus was to clear her mind from her husband, who she left in Atlanta and was seeking a divorce.

It wasn't until he pulled up with her and stared at the luxurious mansion in awe that he realized that April was the jackpot. He further inquired about her life and learned that she was a swimsuit model. With that revelation, Vibe planned to milk the cow until it went dry.

Vibe was a six one, dark-skinned nigga with twelve 22-karat golds in his mouth, six on top of the other. His mother, Erica, was from College Park, and everyone knew her as a godly woman, while his father, Jr., resided in Florida. He was a real cocaine dealer, who had the streets in Martin County on lock.

"Baby, I'm cumming!" she screamed as Vibe pounded her hard and mercilessly.

Damn, this cracker got some good-ass pussy, and she knows how to work . . . !

"Oh shit!" Vibe yelled out as he came to his load inside his Trojan condom.

"Damn it! That was great!" April exclaimed.

"There's more of that where that came from," Vibe retorted breathlessly as he lay in the bed.

"I bet, and I will want some later," she said as she walked to the bathroom.

In mid-stride, she stopped and caught Vibe mesmerized at her curves.

"Are you coming to join me?" April asked while rubbing her ass.

"Damn right!" Vibe exclaimed as he then leaped from the comfortable king-size bed.

Inside the steam shower, Vibe fucked her again like a sex maniac in hopes of sealing his fate with the gorgeous model.

All I have to do is fuck this bitch's brains out and make her divorce that cracker, Vibe plotted as he penetrated her deeply.

"You mind me, huh?" Vibe said to April while nailing her from the back. "Do you mind me, I say?" he yelled out, demanding an answer from her, whose mouth was wide open and caught up in ecstasy.

"Yes! Yes! Vibe, I mind you!" she said breathlessly.

"This is my pussy. Do you mind me taking over, huh?" he asked.

"Yes! Vibe, your pussy!" she screamed out.

"Arrgghh! Uhhh!" the both of them came together to electrifying orgasms.

"Shit!" Vibe exclaimed as he released his load on her back.

He was hooked on something new. Never in his twenty-four years had he made love to a white woman.

I see why niggas who dipped their dicks in milk went crazy. This shit got its own flavor. But it will never be as good as a sista, he thought, exhausted.

* * *

Shaquana was on her way to school in her new-model Monte Carlo, the color of Champagne, with 24-inch Fury rims and a thunderous bass system. She was playing a new song by Fantasia, and she was in good spirits. When she came upon a red light at an intersection, she turned down the volume and serenaded to the lyrics emanating from her four 12-inch speakers and 6 x 9s made by Sony.

Where the fuck is Champagne? Shaquana pondered about her friend, who she had last talked with over three weeks ago. *Almost a damn month!* she thought as she pulled out her iPhone and dialed Champagne's number for the umpteenth time.

But just like every time since Champagne's phone died on her, the phone rang until it went to voicemail: "Hello! Who this? Oh well, check it . . ."

Shaquana quickly hung up, refusing to listen to Champagne's deceitful voicemail, and proceeded through the green light.

This is so not like Champagne. That bitch holding back on something . . . like what? she thought.

Five

"And our next player is a number six draft and a CFL player, who's had a wonderful year as a linebacker and is essentially needed in the NFL. For the Dallas Cowboys, people . . . give it up for Jerome Wilkins . . . #18!" the NFL draft host announced to the crowd.

Jerome strutted up to the stage and accepted his Cowboys jersey, becoming an official Cowboy. He then spoke into the microphone at the podium once the cheering and whistling came to a sudden halt.

"Thank you all, for without our fans and support, this wouldn't be possible. This sport is a life-teaching experience to me and has helped me deal with some tough situations. I'm glad that I stayed strong and got through it all. Now I have to keep my fans happy and just play great," Jerome said as he threw up his massive muscular arms to the crowd, which broke into an ovation.

Brenda turned the television off and sat in the darkness in her living room. She was glad for her ex, but hurt from missing him.

He'll never understand walking in on his bitch while she was getting the shit fucked out of her.

"No man or woman could put forth an understanding," Brenda said to herself.

She seriously wanted to kill Goodman for showing up to her house unexpected, but she knew that it took two to mingle. And that day, Jerome had walked in on her and

Goodman fucking, and there were two careless motherfuckers mingling.

How stupid! Brenda thought. She was lonesome lately and had no one to come assuage her pain and anguish. She was sexually overdue and only had one person in mind, but could she do it? was her self-inquiry.

No! I can't. Hell no! Brenda immediately thought, dismissing the grimy prospect from her mind. Brenda lay back on her leather sofa in her silk gown and closed her eyes to prevent an inevitable flow of tears.

Any man could look at her and see how hurt she was, but there wasn't any man available to hold her in his arms, if that's all he did.

Someone like . . . Maurice, she thought before she began to shake her head from side to side, gesturing an indication of no.

It didn't matter how much she'd tried to dismiss sleeping with him from her mind. He'd always return.

Brenda turned on her side and cuddled one of the sofa's pillows and then closed her eyes to catch some rest and attempt to sleep the frustration of lonesomeness away. Before she drifted off to sleep, she thought of her and Jerome's good times together, but she finally found herself thinking about Maurice—a man her soul was yearning for.

* * *

"K-Zoe! Don't play with me! Why the fuck is this ho all in your face, huh?" Coco yelled at him outside Cub Liv in Miami.

When Coco had seen the dark-skinned woman wearing

29

next to nothing in K-Zoe's face and smiling seductively, Co-co invaded and told the woman to step back or get stepped on.

Since leaving Georgia with K-Zoe to lay low from Big Dee's murder, the two of them had become close and more than just fucking mates. She loved everything about him, and he was giving her some extraordinary affection. The stripper life was gone from her, and she had become Tameka's setup girl on call and homegirl to trust. When she came to Miami, she quickly learned that K-Zoe was a damn womanizer, and it killed her to see another woman in his grill, because her feelings for him were blooming at every moment he was with her. And when he was away, it would kill her just to know that he was out in the world among other bitches.

"K-Zoe! I'm not playing. Why you got that ho in your face?" she asked, looking up at him with a pout on her lips and her hands on her hips.

"Baby, that woman means no harm. She's business. Turn down a little. Okay?" K-Zoe spoke in his heavy Haitian accent that made Coco wet between her legs every time.

"It's always business. Don't play me, K-Zoe. Niggas don't know what's good until it's gone . . ."

Before she could finish, K-Zoe grabbed her into his arms and forced a strong kiss on her mouth. At first she tried to resist, but she quickly yielded at the sweet comfort that had always gotten her attention.

K-Zoe kissed her in front of everyone who was entering and leaving the club, letting every nigga and bitch know that Coco was his. She tried to run when he started to kiss her on her neck, because she knew that he was trying to freak her in public now.

"Stop, K-Zoe!" she yelled while laughing, unable to resist him as he planted his mouth on her neck and started sucking.

"Damn, baby!" she purred out, slightly arching her back. "Baby, let's go!" she exclaimed, all hot and horny.

"Woman! This is not business; it's my feelings! Please don't worry about these hos out here, because K-Zoe could have had 'em all. But I chose you, beautiful. Look around! They all see!" K-Zoe said, spinning Coco around as she saw the entire club locked on them. She felt like the special lady she was, and K-Zoe had done a presidential performance to prove it to her as well.

She was touched by how well he conveyed his feelings, and knew that she'd found her man in life. And all she wanted to do at that moment was take him home.

"Baby, can we go now?" she said, looking at him with a seductive look on her face.

"I was just about to ask you the same thing," K-Zoe retorted as he grabbed Coco around her thin waist and departed the club with his queen that he was ready to give his all.

* * *

When Tameka pulled up to the $1.5 million mansion in North Miami, she felt like the boss she was. D-Zoe was in the backseat with her in the luxurious limo, and they were there to visit an important individual. When the limousine halted in front of the mansion's front door, two muscular Haitian men opened the back door and allowed Tameka to step out, with D-Zoe behind her.

"Good morning, Meka," one of the men said to her as he helped her out of the car.

"Good morning, Jean," Tameka responded as she waited for D-Zoe to be patted down by the other man.

Despite Tameka being Haitian Beny's second-in-command, anyone rolling with her wasn't exempt from the cautionary examination.

"I hope that you enjoy yourself, Meka," Jean said, trying his best to sound sexy to her in front of D-Zoe.

D-Zoe looked at Jean and shot an insult off to him in Creole.

Tameka could sense the tension and stepped in to pull D-Zoe out of Jean's face, who was laughing and unmoved by the insult.

"Come, D-Zoe. Now!" Tameka said, pulling him by the arm and away from the six foot four Jean.

Niggas ready to die over pussy that ain't even theirs. Neither one of them got a ring on my finger! Tameka thought as she stormed into the mansion.

When she and D-Zoe headed up the staircase, her anticipation had intensified. At the end of the hall, on the second floor, on the right was a guest room the size of a master bedroom, with a luxurious hot tub inside. Tameka stuck a key inside the knobless door and pushed it open. When she and D-Zoe entered the opulent room, they both heard the cries of Champagne cuddling her plush pillows, unaware of their presence.

"Less crying and more paying attention to your surroundings! Last time I could remember, this is what made you unable to sense the smell of danger," Tameka said, startling Champagne, who jumped up from lying on the bed at the sound of Tameka's voice.

When she looked past Tameka, she saw D-Zoe sitting in an antique leather chair in the corner of the room.

"What do you want from me?" Champagne said, sniveling and wiping her bloodshot eyes from excessive crying.

"Baby girl . . . there's a lot I want from you. You see, at first I just wanted to talk to you. You know . . . like woman to woman."

"About what? Are you Jarvis's wife? Because if you are, I swear that I had no clue that he was married. I just want to go home, please," Champagne pleaded.

Married to that bastard! Be for real, bitch! All this shit would be bloody red if you were supposedly the mistress! Tameka thought as she walked closer to Champagne and sat down on the bed next to her.

Champagne was perplexed and afraid of Tameka, but she refused to reveal her fear despite Tameka being able to smell the intensity of it.

"Come here, 'Pagne. I'm not going to hurt you," Tameka said while patting the empty space between them.

Champagne was reluctant at first, and then she reminded herself that she wouldn't show any fear. When she came closer, Tameka sighed and then spoke.

"Jarvis is in some serious trouble, and I'm afraid that you are too, Champagne."

"He and I have done nothing wrong to anybody. You're my boss. Is this because of how he hurt you?" Champagne asked. "Because you may not remember, but I stopped him from further harming you. It was wrong what he did," she continued as she watched D-Zoe still sitting emotionless in the chair.

33

"No! This is far beyond what you would have ever expected 'Pagne, and all I want to know is why did you do it . . . if she was your friend? And tell me why I should spare you?" Tameka asked.

What is she talking about? Champagne wanted to know, deeply confused.

"Can you be clear to me? What are we talking about . . . ?"

Smack!

"Bitch! Don't play games with me now. If we're going to play these games, just tell me, so I can beat you at them. Because you will never win, bitch!" Tameka yelled in a raging fit after slapping Champagne hard in her face and splitting open her lip.

Tameka watched as the blood formed on her bottom lip, yet she felt no remorse whatsoever.

"Benjamin . . . !"

Oh my God! Champagne thought when Tameka spoke his name.

"He was a friend of ours, and I'm sure that we're on the right path of understanding now. For some reason, my gut tells me that Jarvis's master plan was to kill Benjamin to get to what he had. I thought it was me . . . until I learned of you and your grimy cutthroat traits. How could you kill your friend's mother over a man that was neither of ours? Jarvis tricked me, and it's time for us to trick him. Are you down, or is this your predestined fate . . . to die after I kill him?"

Girl, go with the flow! Champagne's inner voice told her.

"I'm down," she answered.

Six

Most people mistook him as a negro, when in fact he was considered a Cuban negro. Black Cuban stood five seven and sported a clean-shaven bald head and facial hair. He was very dark-skinned and rocked one shiny 22-karat gold on his left top canine tooth. At forty-three years old, he was the face of the Miami drug world and had an impenetrable organized drug distribution. The feds were desperately trying to bring him down, but they failed at every attempt and in most cases lost their lives. But there was no evidence to link Cuban Black to the preposterous murder rate in Miami.

He lived in North Miami in a $3.5 million mansion, with three wives who lived under the same roof and made love to him at the same time. He was an Old Testament believer and looked up to King David. He felt that King David was the real epitome of a pimp, and that Solomon was the smartest nigga ever to be alive and walk the earth, other than Jesus.

Cuban Black was out back by his pool enjoying the company of his three wives, all of whom were under thirty. They were all wearing identical red satin bikinis and caressing their man, massaging his body and rubbing him down with oil. He was sore from his intense workout that he did earlier in the day in his home gym. Despite his age, Cuban Black was in great shape and built on the stocky side. With all three of his wives, he shared a son who had a striking resemblance to him.

Tatanisha was a swarthy, gorgeous twenty-five-year-old, who was his first wife—and number one among the three. Mercedes, was a twenty-two-year-old, brown-skinned model. Cuban Black had snatched her from her career and made her his second wife. His third wife was from his native Cuba. She was a gorgeous twenty-eight-year-old woman named Selena Rodriguez, who favored Gina Rodriguez and often was mistaken for her.

He loved them all equally and would kill anyone who harmed them or looked as if they wanted to harm them. Despite their positions, they were all aware that he was still mingling with other women. Although, Cuban Black recently had promised them that he would tone down the outside relationships to protect them all, because disease was everywhere in the world and increasing the death toll every day.

"Yo, Black! You have a phone call," Cuban Black's lieutenant, Miguel, said as he walked toward him carrying a cordless phone in his hand.

"Who is it?"

"Haitian Beny. He's calling again from the same line," Miguel retorted, informing Cuban Black that Beny was calling from a cell phone that Cuban Black had smuggled in to a correctional officer who was on his payroll to take care of Haitian Beny. Beny was being held in a Georgia federal holding cell until he was scheduled to go to trial or take a deal.

"I'll take it, Miguel. Thanks," Cuban Black said as he sat up and took the phone from his youngest lieutenant, who was only eighteen years old but with a ridiculous body count in the Little Haiti gutters.

"Ladies, please excuse me," he said as he stood up after grabbing the phone and walked over to the end of the pool to speak in private with Beny, who had been a good friend of his for a long time.

"What's up, knucklehead?" Cuban Black said into the phone.

"Same old thing, shawty! What's good with you?" Haitian Beny asked.

"You should have the $20,000 on your books tomorrow," Cuban Black told him.

"Thanks, man, I really appreciate that. Because these swines have everything in their hands, and I can't make no more across seas," Beny explained.

"Yeah, that's a sticky situation. Listen . . . I'm glad that you called. I want to see what's up with your second-in-command. I've been watching her close and see that she knows how to move with caution, and she's even passed a couple of my tests. So, most definitely, I want to meet her as soon as possible," Cuban Black said.

"You give me the date and time, and I'll make sure she's there," Haitian Beny said.

"Perfect! How about three weeks. Tell her to show up at the Hilton and ask for David Gomez . . ."

"Which Hilton?"

"Downtown Atlanta," Cuban Black responded.

"Okay, I will do it. They're about to walk through and do count. I'll hit you up in a couple days, shawty," Beny said.

"Okay, do that playa . . ."

"Love."

"Love," Cuban Black replied as they hung up the phone.

I told that nigga to slow down, and just like twelve years ago, he fumbled, Cuban Black reflected as he walked back to his wives and lay back down in the beach chair.

"Baby . . . are you thirsty?" Tatanisha asked him while resuming rubbing her delicate hands across his back.

"Yeah. Get me some iced tea, baby," he said.

"Mercedes, go handle that for daddy," Tatanisha commanded her, since she was the head wife and whatever she said was to be followed immediately, just like her husband's potency.

"Yes, ma'am," Mercedes said as she strutted inside to get her husband some iced tea.

"It'll be here in no time, daddy," Tatanisha informed him.

"Thank you, baby gal," Cuban Black said.

* * *

When Haitian Beny got off the phone with Cuban Black, he quickly slid the Verizon flip phone into the confines of his plush pillow that he sat on in his wheelchair, which he was using after being shot in his leg by Agent Norton.

He wheeled himself over to the door and watched the female correctional officer as she walked through for count. He was housed alone and was grateful for the privacy.

"Damn, that bitch know she got a fat ass!" Haitian Beny said while watching the ridiculous ass on CO Johnson, a black woman who thought she was a white woman.

I can't stand a bitch who don't know her worth, Haitian Beny thought as she passed his cell and then backed up further to look inside.

"Back up, inmate, when I'm walking through. You're too close to the door. I don't know if you're playing with yourself or not . . ."

Bitch! Get from my door with that sick shit! he wanted to say, but he held his tongue and wheeled himself away from the door.

She paid close attention to his crotch area, to see if he was some type of pervert who would masturbate to the female guards. When she saw that he wasn't erect, she moved on.

"Bitch! You ain't all that!" one of the inmates called out to her as she continued to do her walk.

"Ho-ass nigga! Whoever you is . . . put your cellmate's dick back in your mouth!" Johnson yelled back at the insult, receiving a wing full of laughs and oohs.

When she was gone, Haitian Beny dug out his phone again and called Tameka's number. At first he was skeptical of letting her be his second-in-command, but he knew the chances of letting a nigga carry him. He'd dealt with disloyal men, who were only loyal to the money. So he took his chances with a woman—a lethal, maniacal woman. When Tameka didn't pick up, he called D-Zoe.

I'm glad I put Tameka in charge. Shit! I may be gone for the long ride, and a nigga wasn't about to keep it real with Beny, he thought to himself as D-Zoe answered.

"Hello!"

"What's up, Haitian?" Beny said to D-Zoe in Creole.

"Good. What about you?"

"Where's Meka?"

"She's in the shower. I'll have her hit ya back when—"

"Okay, tell her I will hit her back. Don't never call me. This shit ain't legal," Haitian Beny said to D-Zoe, who seemed ingenuous to illegal cellular devices in prison.

"Okay, brah. Ummm . . . do that!" D-Zoe said.

"How's K-Zoe?" Beny asked.

"He's the same Beny . . . club . . . club . . . club!"

"Is he doing what he needs to do, Haitian?" Beny asked with concern.

"Baby, can you bring me a towel, please?"

Baby! These bitches fucking. D-Zoe know how I feel about that shit! Beny thought.

"Okay, hold on . . ."

"Yo, D-Zoe! Are you and Meka fucking?"

D-Zoe knew that Haitian Beny didn't operate business with pleasure, despite the many times that Beny himself wanted to explore Tameka.

"I'm talking to you, man. Are you two fucking, D-Zoe?" Haitian Beny asked sternly.

"Man! Beny . . . you worried about the wrong thing in the wrong position. Getting out of that shit should be your worries, not who I'm fucking . . . !"

"Motherfucker! I raised your ass. You have no right to talk crazy to me!" Beny exclaimed in a loud whisper.

"Tameka . . . phone!" D-Zoe said as he walked into the bathroom with the towel that she had requested and handed her the phone.

"Who?" she asked, perplexed.

"Beny!" he responded angrily.

"What's wrong, baby?" Tameka said, seeing the frustration on D-Zoe's face.

"Your partner too worried about us rather than his freedom. You deal with him!" D-Zoe said as he walked out of the bathroom.

"Hello," she answered.

"Meka, please listen to me. Black wants to see you next week at the Hilton in downtown Atlanta. You are to ask for a David Gomez, walk to the room, and there you will meet him," Beny said with a sigh.

"Another thing, Meka . . . I can't get on you about it because I never established it among us two. But D-Zoe knows my rules . . . as a team player, we are not to have any sexual—"

"Hello . . . Meka?" Beny called out to the dead line.

I know this bitch didn't hang up! he thought.

* * *

Fuck he think he is . . . some Mafia boss nigga? Meka going to fuck whoever she pleases! Fuck Beny! You are not my man or daddy! Tameka thought as she walked into the room and found D-Zoe sitting on the bed with his hands covering his face. He was worried and looked like a man who had broken a pact with his friend.

"He's not in control of us or you no more!" she said to D-Zoe while standing in front of him, wrapped in a plush, pink towel.

"Do you hear me?" she asked, lifting his head up to stare into his eyes.

I'm about to be the diva of the South, she thought.

"Yeah, I hear you."

"Good. Now make love to me!" she commanded.

Seven

Ms. Mae was sitting in her favorite rocking chair, humming to an old-school classic jazz hit with her eyes closed, when the knocks came at her front door. Her eyes opened up, and she saw two figures standing outside her screen door. Her vision was blurry, making her unable to see who it was.

"Who is there?" Ms. Mae called.

"Jonesboro Police. We're here for a Champagne Robinson. We would like to speak with her," a female voice said.

"Wait a minute! I'm coming," Ms. Mae said as she got up out of her chair, grabbed her cane, and walked over to the door.

When she opened the door, she saw a white female police officer and a white male officer in plain clothes.

"You're looking for my granddaughter? Me too!" Ms. Mae exclaimed.

"Ma'am, we're here to speak with her . . ."

"And like I told you, I haven't seen her in weeks," Ms. Mae replied.

"Isn't this where she resides?" the female officer asked.

"Yes, she does, but the last time I checked . . . Is she in some trouble?"

"Well, we're investigating a murder that recently happened at Pleasers."

"That strip club that I hear she's been working at?"

"Yes, ma'am. She happens to have been an employee there, and we're in the midst of questioning everyone. Is there any way we could get in immediate contact with her?" the male officer asked.

"Ummm . . . her friend, Shaquana Clark . . . maybe she could tell you where that heifer's been hiding at," Ms. Mae said, causing both officers to laugh lightly.

"How do we get in contact with Shaquana Clark? Wait a minute! Is this the sister of Daquan Clark?"

"And daughter of Benjamin and Renae Clark," Ms. Mae retorted to the female officer.

The female officer pulled out a small notepad and pen and began taking her notes.

"Where could we find Shaquana? I'm sure that we won't be able to find her at their burned down residence," she said.

"I bet you won't either. But I think her Auntie Brenda, who stays on 19th Street, could assist you with more information," Ms. Mae said.

"You said 19th Street. Do you know what house she lives in?" the male officer asked.

"The beautiful house. It's the one that sticks out among them all."

"Thank you, ma'am, for your cooperation,"

"There's something going on I just can't put my finger on . . . other than that heifer stealing my checks. I should put her ass in jail. She's lucky that I'm from the old school and know how to handle mines," Ms. Mae said to herself as she walked back into her home and resumed humming in her rocking chair.

She will pay for her betrayal. I raised that woman too good for her to steal from me, Ms. Mae contemplated, deeply hurt by Champagne's actions of stealing from the blind.

* * *

"Okay, people! Remember . . . tomorrow is an exam. Then we're moving on to phase two. Please be considerate of yourselves and get plenty of rest. Class dismissed!" the Italian teacher announced to her class of fifty.

Shaquana was among them at the special alternative school where dropouts came to finish their education and receive their high school diploma. Everyone there was serious about obtaining an education and wanted to seek further career plans.

Shaquana gathered up her books and walked out of the building in a hurry, to get out of the hot sun. As she got to her Monte Carlo, someone called her name.

"Shaquana! Wait up a second!" a man's voice called out.

When she turned around and removed her Gucci shades, she was staring at the handsome man who sat in her row behind her in class.

What she was wondering was, *How the fuck does he know my name, when Shaquana doesn't fuck with nobody at adult-aid education?*

"Yes. How may I help you?" she asked.

He was a clean-shaven, low-face-wearing, pecan handsome man in his early twenties, who stood five eight and weighed 160 pounds.

Too damn handsome! she thought.

"Sorry to bother you, but my name is Kenneth, and I was just wondering if I could pay you for a lift to College Park."

Really! Shaquana thought, since their school was in East Atlanta, where she and Maurice lived together, and she really didn't want to be driving across town, especially with a strange classmate.

Shaquana looked at him and sighed. "Kenneth . . . how did you get here?" she asked him.

"My baby momma dropped me off, shawty. Now she can't because the police just grabbed her and are threatening to take away my kids."

"Like I told you, I'm willing to pay you whatever," Kenneth said, reaching into his pocket to retrieve a hefty wad of cash.

Nigga! I don't need your money! she thought as he peeled off $500 and attempted to hand it to her.

Shaquana stared, dumbfounded, and began: "Kenneth . . ."

"Call me Ken."

"Ken. Okay . . . well, I don't need your money, and I would normally not do this. The only reason I'm saying yes is for your kids. Let's go!" she said as she strutted over to the driver's seat.

Kenneth stood for a second and admired her curvaceous body that was accentuated through her jersey dress that matched her NFL Jets cap on her head.

Damn! This bitch is jazzy and gorgeous! he thought as he walked toward the passenger side of her car and got in.

Once inside, Shaquana had to pull her dress down to keep it from running up her sexy succulent thighs.

When Kenneth looked at her photo on the dashboard, he saw her hugging on a man that he knew.

Damn, this one of Maurice's bitches! he thought.

As Shaquana navigated out of the parking lot, K. Michelle emanated from her car system and vibrated the seats and windows.

"Say you can't raise a man!" Shaquana sang along, serenading to K. Michelle's lyrics.

Kenneth thought she had a beautiful voice as well, and he decided to kill their silence to build some level of rapport between them.

As he reached for the radio, Shaquana slapped his hand away.

Smack!

"Oww!" Kenneth screamed out in feigned pain while fanning his hand.

Shaquana reached out and turned down the volume herself while laughing at his acting.

"Nigga, you know the rules. Never touch a black woman's radio . . . And what's your career of choice? I hope not acting, because you suck!" Shaquana said to him, still finding him amusing.

"Nah! It's not acting. I was thinking about law school . . ."

"Oh my God! Seriously? What type of law?" she asked ecstatically.

She thought she was the only person with an interest in pursuing the field of law, but she was wrong.

"I don't know. I'm kind of indecisive at the moment," Kenneth said as Shaquana hopped on the interstate and accelerated toward College Park.

"So, you have a great voice, and I thought that singing would be your career choice until . . . you got excited a moment ago. So tell me . . . what part of law you seeking to follow up on?" he asked her.

"Umm . . . law enforcement . . ."

Damn, she flat out told me with no problems. Why can't I tell her the same? Kenneth thought.

He as well wanted to be a part of law enforcement and stop all the killers and drugs from expanding into the gutters.

But how could she want to be a police officer while her man was a damn drug lord predestined to fall? Kenneth pondered angrily.

"Is that a problem? Why you get quiet?" Shaquana asked, sensing the discomfort in his sudden change of demeanor.

"Nah! It's not a problem to be what you want, gorgeous . . ."

"Please, no compliments, but thanks. But I have a man."

"Are you two married?" he asked.

How the hell we jumped subjects? she wondered.

"Sorry," he said, now sensing her discomfort.

"It's okay. No . . . we're not married. But he holds my heart, and I have respect for him," she explained.

"I didn't want to tell you because I didn't want you to look at me like a busta. But I'm interested in joining the DEA . . ."

"Damn!" Shaquana shrieked.

"What?" Kenneth asked.

"Nothing! It's just, you never know what other people's concerns are until you ask. I want to become a detective and find the people who killed my parents," Shaquana explained, holding back a flood of tears.

Please don't cry, she told herself internally.

"Sorry to hear that," Kenneth said, placing his hands on her shoulder.

When she flinched, he quickly removed his hand, realizing that he was overdoing things.

"I'm sorry, Shaquana," he said.

For a moment, she was quiet and had turned off the interstate, coasting into the city limits of College Park.

"It's okay. I understand, Ken. You were just being a man, and I appreciate that. Now, where to . . . ?"

"The hood on 9th . . ."

"The hood on 9th?"

Oh shit! What if I run into Maurice? I'm only giving my classmate a ride home, she thought, quickly assuaging her anguish.

When she turned into the hood on MLK Boulevard, she got to 9th as fast as she could. She was grateful not to see her man's Navigator pulling off any of the adjacent streets.

When Kenneth directed her to his apartment complex, she sighed a breath of relief from being so paranoid.

"Thanks a lot, Shaquana. I'll see you tomorrow. Maybe we can talk more on our career options. For some reason, I feel good letting a stranger know my desire and not being judged as a bastard!" he said as he stepped out of her car.

"I'll see you tomorrow, and never worry about what people think of you. All that matters is what you think," Shaquana said.

"That's true. Thanks . . . and drive safe," Kenneth said as he closed the door.

When Shaquana pulled off, she was happy to be rid of him, not because of his handsomeness, but because of what Maurice would think if he caught a fine-ass nigga in her car.

What the fuck was I thinking? she thought as she accelerated out of College Park's hood.

*   *   *

When D-Rock saw Shaquana's car parked out in front of Building H, he thought that it was Maurice pulling up unannounced like he had done before. But when he saw the nigga step out, he was perplexed and angry for his cousin. He wasted no time pulling out his iPhone and recording the unbelievable sight of his cousin's bitch dropping off a nigga from his own hood—and a nigga who was known to fuck his homeboy's bitches.

"Skank-ass ho!" D-Rock exclaimed, badly wanting to pull his Glock .17 from underneath his shirt and pop Kenneth and Shaquana, and then leave them for Maurice to see.

Instead, he played it cool and watched her pull off in a hurry and then Ken walk toward his complex mirthfully. It was Shaquana, too, no doubt, because no one owned a car like hers. It was unique in Atlanta, and last, there was the irrefutable embellished nametag on the grill that read "Shaquana 'n' Maurice—Don't Hate."

"These hos ain't loyal. Don't matter how good you treat them," D-Rock said as he called Maurice to deliver him the news of his skank bitch.

Eight

When Shaquana made it home, she saw all three of Maurice's cars in the parking lot.

Damn! He's home. This will be a first, she thought as she walked inside the high-rise building. When she took the elevator up to their suite, a thought triggered in her head out of nowhere.

How come Kenneth didn't have a cab if he had money to take one . . . niggas! she considered as the elevator reached her floor.

When she made it to the opulent suite and allowed herself in, the smell of marijuana redolently lingered in the suite's atmosphere.

I hate that shit! A home is supposed to smell like a home when walking inside, Shaquana thought.

"Maurice!" she screamed out as she passed through the suite's vestibule.

When she made it the living room, she found him sitting on the leather sofa with his legs stretched out on the glass table.

"Damn, baby. You didn't hear me calling you?" Shaquana asked as she walked over to him, simultaneously removing her large gold elephant earrings and tossing them on the table.

When she looked at the TV, she saw that it was on mute, and the room became eerie when Maurice still remained silent after she'd asked him a question. She immediately sensed something wrong.

"Maurice . . . are you okay?" she asked as she came closer, climbed into his lap, and put her arms around his neck.

Maurice admired her in her jersey dress and how delicious she was looking. It angered him and hurt him deeply to imagine his baby stepping out on him, especially with a nigga from his hood.

"What's wrong, baby?" she asked him again, holding her face up to look into his eyes.

What she saw was ineffable and disturbing. It was something she had never seen before in them before.

"I'm okay. Just got a lot on my mind, baby," he said.

"Like what?" she asked.

Like you fucking behind my back! Maurice wanted to say, but he just smiled and said, "It's a street thang, shawty. No pressure."

"Oh really?" Shaquana said, knowing Maurice well enough to know he wouldn't be worried about anything in the streets. But her being her, she wouldn't push the issue.

Maurice's smile did cheer things up for her, despite the little discomfort that remained in the air.

"So, tell me . . . how was your day at school?" Maurice asked, caressing her ass while looking in her eyes.

I drove this sexy nigga home, who I found I have a common desire with to join the law . . . is what Shaquana couldn't tell Maurice, although she felt that she should tell him.

Instead she sighed and said, "School was normal. I have to take an exam tomorrow, and I have one more phase to take until I graduate."

"That's good, baby!" Maurice exclaimed in feigned excitement. "What hotshot is passing you love notes?" he then asked.

"Boy . . . ain't nobody passing me any love notes!" she retorted.

"Come on, baby. Keep it real. You're a bad baby, and fly at that, so no man is cutting his eyes?" Maurice asked.

"Baby, I don't even conversate with any man or woman in my class. I come and get my work done and then come home," she said.

"Would you tell me?" Maurice asked.

"Of course I will, baby . . ."

Then tell him about Kenneth! her soul screamed out.

"I know you would, baby," Maurice said as he then kissed her softly on her lips.

"I love you, Maurice . . ."

No you don't, bitch! You have no clue what love is. Love is when you can be real with your man . . . and not step out on him! Maurice wanted to tell Shaquana.

Instead, he played it cool and said, "I love you more than you'll ever imagine. Just know that there's only one door to walk in."

Maurice pointed at his chest, letting her know that it was one way into his heart. And when it was broken by infidelity—like once before, with his first love, Amber—he dealt with the pain unlike others would.

"I know, Maurice. I care so much about you," she said.

If you did, bitch, you wouldn't be creeping on me! Maurice thought.

"And I care about you too," he said, but not from the same prospect as Shaquana.

He made love to her and put her to sleep like always. And as usual, when she awoke, he was gone.

Damn! I love this man, she thought as she drifted back to sleep.

When she saw Kenneth looking at her smiling, she immediately blushed.

"Come here, shawty!" Kenneth said as she walked toward him, hugging her books against her chest.

They were the only two in the hallway, and she could see the lust in his eyes. It made her become wet between her legs, and she badly wanted to sample his way of loving. But she couldn't. Her man was Maurice.

As she continued to walk toward Kenneth, she heard Maurice's voice: "You lied to me!"

"Oh my God!" Shaquana exclaimed as she woke from her dream sweaty and with her heart beating rapidly.

I can't! What is going on? Why the fuck am I dreaming about another man? Shaquana wanted to know, but she had no way to answer nature's doings.

Shaquana got out of bed and took a long, steaming shower to soothe her guilty conscience.

Damn! But I didn't do nothing. Why do I feel as if I did? she asked herself.

* * *

When Romel saw the two FBI agents walk into the room, his face instantly frowned up in hatred at the sight of Markeina.

I can't believe this ho is a fucking fed. How could I have not seen it? he reflected.

He was restrained by a belly chain and ankle shackles to prohibit him from attacking his enemies.

"How are you doing, Romel?" Clemons spoke while taking a seat at the round table, with a brown folder clutched in her hands. She wore an expensive suit revealing her badge and weapon on her waist. Behind her stood her partner.

Who is this George Clooney lookalike motherfucker? Romel wanted to know as he observed Agent Norton.

"What do you want, Mar—"

"That's not my name, Romel. Please call me Agent Clemons. I'm sure you already know this . . ."

Is this bitch getting offended at her own scam? Romel thought, almost revealing a chuckle but deciding against it.

He was being held in Valdosta, Georgia, at a federal holding facility, with Big Funk and Corey, and separate from Haitian Beny, who was in Atlanta.

As much as he hated Agent Clemons, to some degree he had a level of respect for her after she saved his life—despite the shit bag that was attached to his lower stomach, for he was unable to move his own bowels. But he was slowly recovering from the attempt on his life.

He was fortunate to have been air-lifted to the emergency room rather than by an ambulance, or else he would have died en route due to the slow traffic. Now he was praying to see the streets again, although he saw no hint of light in his dark situation. There was all the evidence that was gathered against him during Clemons's undercover operation. And the most damaging evidence was his and Haitian Beny's conspiracy to murder Maurice, Antron, and Jarvis.

The bitch planted a bug in my tie to catch our conversation! Romel thought, recalling the night he and Markeina were in Miami at the Marriott on South Beach.

Damn! This bitch is the devil. How could she set up her own culture? Romel desperately wanted to ask her, but he held his peace.

"Romel . . . we're here to ask you a few questions. Before we continue, please be aware that it's for your own good to help yourself out. This is my partner, Special Agent Brandon Norton . . ."

"I don't care who the fuck he is. What's up?"

Smart ass! Norton thought, with his arms crossed and left hand covering his mouth.

"Romel . . . please save the insolence. Y'all niggas kill me with that shit. Be acting like a damn pit bull, but when you see a bear, you tuck your damn tail like a little bitch!" Agent Clemons fired back at Romel, causing a small chuckle to escape Norton's mouth.

"What the fuck is this cracker laughing for, and what makes your black ass better than me, Markeina?" he asked, emphasizing Markeina.

"You're a criminal . . . and she's not, jackass! Now let's move on," Norton informed. "You're in some shit, and you know how it goes. In order to get out of some shit, you have to give up some shit . . ."

"Cracker . . . you crazy!" Romel yelled.

"Do you think Big Funk and Corey are crazy too? Because obviously they're not. Both of them just signed ten years to bring Haitian Beny down . . ."

"How true is this?" Romel asked Clemons, cutting her off.

Agent Clemons quickly went inside the brown folder in her hands and removed two documents, which she slid over to Romel.

Romel saw that they were legit plea deals for Joseph Lewis (aka Big Funk) and Corey Jean. He read the pleas speedily and then sighed.

Damn! These niggas for real, he thought.

"So, what does this have to do with me?" Romel asked Agent Clemons.

"It means that when they testify, you will be sabotaged along with Haitian Beny," she answered convincingly.

"Help yourself and tell us . . . like Big Funk and Corey have already done . . . what role did Jarvis play in killing Benjamin Clark?"

"Man, I don't know shit about that and don't care either . . ."

"Listen, Romel, we know and just want to give you a chance to help yourself out. Haitian Beny thinks you killed Antron like he ordered you to do. We know you didn't, but do we have to show the court that? Hell no!" Norton explained.

"You were told to kidnap Benjamin's daughter, and you were going to do it. That's life itself . . ."

"Fuck you bitches. I'll die before I sing any song . . ."

"Let's go!" Agent Clemons said, leaping from her seat and then making a departure from the room with loud clanking heels.

"You've got her mad, son. Damn!" Agent Norton said as he gathered the documents from Big Funk and Corey's plea deal and then followed his partner's footsteps.

Romel was speechless and didn't like the eerie feeling that she'd just left him with.

Big Funk and Corey have turned state, but not me, Romel thought while shaking his head at the turncloaks.

"Damn it!" he exclaimed.

The feds just didn't play fair, he thought as two guards came to escort him back to his isolation cell.

Nine

Champagne was soaking and relaxing in her soothing hot tub, when she heard the door to her confined room being pushed open.

Damn it! Who is it now? she wanted to know.

She had already eaten, and Tameka wouldn't be back until next week, so she had no idea who it could be. Champagne got up out of the hot tub, soaking wet, and quickly wrapped herself in a plush towel. When she walked out into the room, it was completely dark.

"What the fuck! I didn't cut no lights off," Champagne mumbled, sensing something amiss as she walked out into the darkness.

She froze when she felt a breeze on her back, and then the bathroom lights went out, startling her to death. Someone was definitely in the room with her, her thoughts registered quickly.

"What the fuck. Who is . . . ?"

Before she could finish, a strong hand wrapped around her throat and throttled her until she was unconscious.

Champagne awoke minutes later on the bed, feeling her tight pussy vigorously being ripped apart by an enormous penis. Her mouth was gagged with a sock and silk scarf to muffle her cries of pain. The stranger continued to thrust with powerful and long strokes in and out of her womb. She became numb. She couldn't believe that she was being raped, and although at the moment she was contemporary, she wanted to die to assuage her pain.

Jarvis . . . why? Why Jarvis? she asked herself, blaming her run-in with his villainess on him.

When the man's thrusting came to a minimum, she was experienced enough with sex to realize that he was on the peak of exploding.

And just like she had sensed, the stranger erupted his load inside of her.

"Ahh shit!" the man let out with a Haitian accent. It was the first time he spoke in her presence.

She was surrounded by Haitians in her windowless room, and she was unaware she was in Miami. She had no clue who the mystery man could be either. When he was done, he unloosened the restraints that bound her hands to the bed post. He didn't bother to remove the gag that muffled her cries, because she now had the use of her own two hands. The mystery man hastened from her room and left Champagne alone in the dark.

She was trembling and in pain as she removed the gag from her mouth and pulled the dirty sock from inside. Champagne slowly emerged from the queen-sized bed, wincing in pain from her sore pussy. She had never taken that much dick in her life. It wasn't just the length that was the problem; it was the girth that made her a new pussy. And though the rapist was gone, she could still feel him thrusting nonchalantly inside her womb.

When she found the light switch on the wall, she flicked it on and illuminated the entire room. When she saw the blood stain on the white sheets of her bed, she took her hand and swiped it across her swollen pussy, wincing in pain. When her hand came back with blood, Champagne broke down crying hysterically.

"Nooo! Why me?" she screamed out, falling to her knees. She couldn't believe that she had just been raped with no remorse. Something within her told her that the stranger would return, and she had nothing to fight him off with. The person she loved, she now hated, and she would do whatever it took to make him feel her pain.

"Fuck you, Jarvis! You can't even rescue me!" Champagne screamed out hysterically.

* * *

Daquan and his new cellmate, Joshah, were working out together, going turn for turn on pushups in their cell. For a week straight, after Christopher left—now known as C-Murder—Daquan's cell stayed cellmate-free until Joshah came from the west wing with his buddy, Lamar King. Daquan was surprised when Joshah asked him if he knew Tittyboo. Unbeknownst to Daquan, Joshah knew everything about Daquan. They quickly bonded. Daquan liked the vibe that Joshah put off. At first, Daquan had to get to know him, for he was skeptical about everyone.

"Joshah Bennette . . . you have a lawyer visit. Report to the lawyer's client," a female officer announced over the intercom as he finished his last set.

"Damn! I forgot that he was coming today!" Joshah said breathlessly.

"One thing about a lawyer . . . ," Daquan began while pumping his set. "They bring good news, even when it's bad news!"

"You right about that!" Joshah said, wiping the sweat from his face and torso with his towel.

"It won't be long, shawty. Them crackers don't have no case against you," Daquan said to his cellmate.

"It's all a waiting process," they said in unison as Joshah left to meet his lawyer.

I really like that nigga. I see why he and Tittyboo are friends, Daquan thought as he watched Joshah leave the wing.

When Joshah walked into the room, he saw who he had expected to be awaiting him. Both partners were sitting at a round table, with a smile on their faces.

"How are you doing, Joshah?" Detective Barns asked, with his legs crossed and hands behind his head.

"I'm okay. So how long do I have to do this?" he asked.

"Tell us what you got thus far," Barns said while his partner, Detective Cunniham, pulled out a notepad and pen, ready to document whatever information Joshah had to offer.

Joshah sighed long before he began.

"We talk every night. Three days ago he opened up to me about the murder . . ."

"What did he say?" Barns asked.

Joshah sighed again before he spoke.

"He told me the same thing that Tittyboo told me, except he thought Cindy and T-Zoe were devils . . ."

"So pretty much he says he was hallucinating at the time he killed Cindy and T-Zoe, and that was because of the flaka that Tittyboo gave him, unbeknownst to Daquan, correct?" Detective Barns restated.

"Yeah, that's what he says. He admitted that he felt like he was on some type of drug," Joshah said.

"And you mentioned nothing to Daquan that Tittyboo has told you, did you?" Barns asked.

"Nah. I didn't tell him shit. All he knows is that me and Tittyboo are friends too. So he trusts me," Joshah said.

Detective Cunniham stopped writing abruptly and looked over at Joshah for a moment before she spoke.

"Joshah . . . would you wear a wire and recap all the information you've given us thus far?"

"What type of wire, ma'am?" Joshah asked.

"A small hidden device unnoticeable to the naked eye," she explained.

"How long will it take to let me out?" Joshah questioned.

Detective Cunniham looked over at her partner, for she couldn't answer his question, since it wasn't her call.

"I tell you what, Joshah . . . you get us a tape by wearing a wire, and we will have you home in no time after you've done your job," Barns told him.

He needed Joshah to cooperate. He had Lamar King go in and wear a wire on Tittyboo, and now he needed Daquan on tape.

"Okay, I will do it," Joshah retorted.

* * *

Haitian Beny sat in his cell on lockdown, awaiting count to clear. For the umpteenth time, he'd tried connecting with Tameka, but to no avail. He couldn't believe how she was avoiding his calls, and he became more and more skeptical by the day of her capability to be loyal. Beny was upset with himself for not being wise with paying closer attention to his surroundings.

When he saw that the FBI was on to him again, he wished that he'd followed his first instinct and closed down his operation.

Damn it! Why the fuck didn't I lay low? he asked himself internally while rubbing the stress from his face.

He dug into the pillow that he sat on in his wheelchair and pulled out his flip phone. By memory, he pushed the numbers for Cuban Black and got a consistent ring and then a voice message.

Haitian Beny quickly disconnected the call and tried Tameka's number. As he put the phone to his ear, he saw a correctional officer pass by his cell.

"Oh shit!" he exclaimed lowly, attempting to hide the phone and hoping that the CO didn't see him.

The phone missed the pillow and dropped to the cell floor.

Damn it, man! Beny thought as he tried reaching for the phone.

The CO was named Shake 'em Down Larry, a canine-sniffing-like veteran who busted convicts with illegal contraband almost every day.

And today he'd add Haitian Beny to his list, with the help of inmates sending in tips informing the facility staff that Beny had a cell phone in his possession.

Larry had crept into the wing from another door, walked toward Beny's cell, and seen him with the phone to his ear. He heard the phone hit the ground. As he slowly backtracked to catch Beny, he caught him leaning over his chair and reaching for the phone on the ground.

When Haitian Beny heard the walkie-talkie crackling, he looked up and stared into the redneck's eyes.

Damn! he thought, unable to reach the phone.

Haitian Beny leaped out of his chair and dove on top of the phone like a maniac.

I got to flush this bitch. I can't let 'em get the contacts, Beny told himself as he tried desperately to crawl toward the toilet.

The moment he made it to the toilet and dumped the phone inside, the cell door rolled open, and the redneck correctional officer tackled Beny. Behind him came other officers, followed by backup from sergeants.

"Nice try, St. Clair. But you're too slow. But we'll get you to confinement real fast, buddy," Larry said.

The phone was retrieved from the toilet and was still operable. Even if he had gotten a chance to push the flush button, it wouldn't have mattered, since the water was turned off. It was a hit that had succeeded with the help of other envious inmates. Unbeknownst to Haitian Beny, things were about to turn really hectic for him.

Ten

When Tameka emerged from the Malibu rental, she took in the sweet Georgia night's atmosphere and realized how she had missed the peach state. It wasn't Palm Beach or Miami, but it had become a home to her too, despite the fucked up memories she shared with the state. As she strutted into the Hilton hotel on Atlanta Boulevard, she paid close attention to her surroundings.

One thing about this game is that it plays dirty 24/7, Tameka thought as she approached the front desk.

"May I help you, ma'am?" an employee asked her while checking her out in her sexy Alexander McQueen dress.

His eyes were on her the moment she stepped through the door. She looked at his name tag, and it read "Mack." He was handsome, but she was here for business, not to look for a good fuck. Being that she left D-Zoe in Miami and traveled by herself, her kitty was alone until she returned to Miami.

"I need the room number to David Gomez," she told Mack.

"David Gomez," he repeated, simultaneously typing on the computer.

"Suite 202 on the 19th floor!"

"Thank you," Tameka replied as she then strutted over to the elevators.

Mack watched her succulent ass cheeks bounce at every step she took, and he admired her Coke-bottle frame.

Damn! That's a bad bitch! he thought to himself.

He was praying that she would turn around and catch him checking her out, but she never did.

When Tameka made it to her destination, she knocked on the door and was let in by a handsome man dressed in a Versace suit and showered in Valentino Uomo cologne. His swarthy complexion seemed out of place momentarily, until he spoke.

"Glad to see that you've made it," the man said to her in a Latino accent that sounded so sweet to her.

"Are you Cuban Black?" she asked.

"The one and only, Meka! It's a pleasure to meet you," he said, grabbing her hand and kissing it like a gentleman.

"It's a pleasure to meet you, too, Cuban Black," Tameka said, with a smile, and blushing to the extreme.

"Come . . . and let's go get something to eat, will you?" Cuban Black said, holding his arm out for Tameka to grab. She was reluctant at first, having a sudden surge of bashfulness.

"Okay!" she responded as she grabbed hold of his arm.

Together they walked out of the suite and downstairs like a couple. Passing the front desk, Mack wanted to be in David Gomez's shoes. A luxurious black limousine pulled up in front of them and allowed Cuban Black and Tameka to step inside.

* * *

When Jarvis heard the Georgia Power & Light truck outside, he stormed out in a raging fit and rushed the truck.

"You motherfuckers! Think time ain't of the essence? I been waiting for hours for y'all to come out here and fix my shit!" he screamed to the black muscular driver.

There were four workers altogether in the truck, and he was the only negro among them.

"Sir, you have to take that up with the office. You see this little mic?" the muscular man said, being sardonic by holding up his truck's radio while fanning it side to side. "When they call me, I come, sir."

"Fuck your stupid mic and office! Just get my lights and power back on!" Jarvis yelled out as he then walked away from the truck to let the men do their job.

Jarvis took a look at his neighbors' homes and noticed that he was the only one with his power out. He paid his bills months in advance, so it was an error. Jarvis had no clue that the FBI was moving in on him and planting bugs in his mansion to gather more evidence on him in the Benjamin Clark murder case. All the workers who arrived on the power truck were undercover FBI agents—and Jarvis didn't have the slightest clue. The four men completed their job and installed twelve bugs throughout his mansion, and they then left without a word. He had his lights and power back on, and a new investigation by the FBI began.

* * *

"This is a nice place, Cuban Black. Long as I been out here, I've never known it to be here," Tameka exclaimed.

"It's one of my favorites!" Cuban Black retorted.

They were at a five-star restaurant in downtown Atlanta called Anna's Steak House, where the best steak was served.

On the ride over, Tameka had learned so much about Cuban Black that turned her on, despite knowing that he had three wives. His honesty was blunt and reminded her so much of Benjamin. From his smile and generosity to his benignity, everything reminded her of Benjamin, who was the last man to treat her womanly. But the love of money had stolen her chances of being loved genuinely.

But he was married! she reflected. When she felt Cuban Black's hand touched the top of hers, she flinched.

"Sorry, Cuban . . . !"

"No, baby girl. Don't be sorry. I'm sorry for startling you."

As he spoke, Tameka looked down at his hand. The man was sporting 14-karat rings on each finger and was wearing a diamond and gold Rolex.

He definitely has cake! she knew.

"Look! I see that there's a lot on your mind. I'm in my forties, and I know you're in your twenties, and after tonight, you'll be in a heavy position. You are very beautiful, and I find you sexually attractive. But I'm afraid we will never become that intimate, especially if we plan to work together . . ."

Are you kidding me, nigga? I want to at least get a sample of that handsome chocolate Cuban dick, she contemplated as the waiter set down their steak dinners in front of them.

"Mr. Gomez . . . would you like any other bottle with your Dom Pérignon?" the tall, young black man asked Cuban Black. "It's buy one, get one free tonight, sir."

"Son . . . bring me a bottle of Ace of Spades Rosé . . . When I'm on my way out the door, please," Cuban Black said, with his hand still on top of Tameka's.

Damn! This nigga playing hard to get, huh! Tameka thought.

"I sure will, sir. Have a nice night," the waiter said as he walked away.

They were in a back booth by themselves, which was done intentionally. Cuban Black's baby sister, Anna, owned the restaurant, which was unknown to Tameka. When the waiter left, Cuban Black continued to speak to Tameka while staring directly into her eyes.

"Tameka . . . I want you to be on my team and replace Haitian Beny. He's a long-time friend, but we've shared many differences. He's now in a situation where twelve years would look like a day to him, but unfortunately . . . it'll never happen. He was caught with his cell phone a couple days ago, and I know why you've been dodging his calls . . ."

How the fuck do you know I've been avoiding him? she thought.

"Cuban Black . . . how do you know that?" Tameka asked, with a smirk on her face.

"I know everything about you, woman. And if you weren't built for what I need you for, then we wouldn't even be this close . . . and you wouldn't even know what Cuban Black looks like," he said. "Let's eat, and then we can discuss the importance."

"Cuban Black?" Tameka called out to him.

"Yes, Meka."

"Never say never. Business has its limits. I don't believe being held down by any street-made principles, and if you know me like you've stated, then you know exactly what I mean."

"What do you mean, Tameka? I'm at a loss!" he asked in feigned confusion.

"Let's eat, Cuban Black. We have plenty of time to make history. Just never say never . . . because I don't believe in it!" she informed.

"What is it that you believe in, Tameka?" he asked her while cutting his steak.

"I believe that if I like it and I want it . . . then I got it," Tameka retorted as she stuffed her mouth with a nice juicy piece of steak.

* * *

When Shaquana pulled up to her auntie's house, she saw two detectives standing at her door talking to Brenda.

What the hell do they want? Shaquana thought as she stepped out of her Monte Carlo and walked toward the front door, where she saw a black woman and white man standing side by side questioning Brenda.

"There's my niece there. Maybe she can assist you," Brenda said, turning the hounds on Shaquana.

"What's the problem, Auntie?" she asked.

"These FBI agents are trying to locate Champagne . . ."

"Aren't we all?" Shaquana retorted.

"Shaquana . . . my name is Agent Clarissa Clemons, and this is my partner, Agent Brandon Norton. Our reasons and concerns to locate Champagne are to speak with her about her boyfriend. We believe that he is somehow involved with your father's murder . . ."

Ain't this some shit! Shaquana thought.

"And this suspicion comes from reliable sources. On the other hand, we also want to question her about a murder that occurred at Pleasers a couple months ago," Clemons continued.

"I'm sorry, but I haven't heard from her in almost two months . . ."

"When was the last time you two talked?" Clemons asked.

"Like I said . . . almost two months ago. Her phone went dead, and she never picked back up," Shaquana told them.

"Did she call you back?"

"No!" Shaquana retorted, shaking her head from side to side.

"Are you two fighting at the moment? You know, homegirl . . . fallout?" Clemons asked.

"No, we are straight last I checked," she answered.

"Does she live with Jarvis? If not him or her grandmother, then where would she disappear to?"

"I have no clue. Do you know where Jarvis stays?" Shaquana asked.

"Yes, we do, but unfortunately Champagne isn't there. We're getting a ping on her phone being at the location of Jarvis's mansion, but she isn't there," Clemons added.

"That's not Champagne to go anywhere without her phone," Shaquana stated.

"Are you sure?" Norton asked.

"Positive!" both Brenda and Shaquana said together.

"Let's go!" Agent Clemons said as the two agents made a dash for her unmarked Yukon SUV while speaking into her radio.

"5012 reporting an AMBER alert on a Champagne Robinson. Requesting all available at Pine Road in Bankhead

2132. I repeat . . . all available . . . move with precaution!" Clemons fired away into her radio.

Shaquana and Brenda watched as the two FBI agents accelerated hastily from Brenda's home to go see about Champagne.

"Something isn't right, Shaquana," Brenda said.

"I just hope that she's alright," Shaquana responded, scared for her friend's well-being, and grateful that she wasn't the only one who suspected Jarvis in her father's murder.

Eleven

Jarvis was sitting at his mini bar in his home, highly intoxicated from his heavy drinking. He was thinking of how he would come across a half billion dollars, when he didn't have nearly a quarter of that amount.

The club was down, and his hip-hop star had been gunned down by an unknown assassin. Big Dee was murdered, and he was constantly being harassed by the authorities. He thought of only one person who could help him with what he had on his mind to get his baby back safely.

Spin! Jarvis thought.

But he had run Spin off from doing business with him when he declined to spot him one hundred kilos of cocaine.

"We've been washing each other's backs" was what Spin had last told him, and he threw the meaningful truth over his shoulders and stomped on it nonchalantly.

Jarvis knew that Spin walked away offended by the refusal to extend his product, and he now wished that he could turn the tables around to make a better difference today.

"Because now, I need Spin more than anything in the world," Jarvis mumbled out to himself.

The city wanted him to shut down the club, and he was looking for the next best rapper to make him a bigger dollar sign.

"I can't believe this bitch wants a half billion dollars, something that the bitch knows I don't have!" Jarvis said sluggishly.

While he was still waiting for Tameka to call, he had been recruiting new men to hold his back down when her wrath did come. Haitian Beny was incarcerated, but he was still skeptical of who his enemies were.

"Man . . . I need to get up with Spin and at least be ready, so when Tameka do call back . . . ," Jarvis mumbled as he walked from the bar into his living room.

As soon as he sat down on the sofa, the power in his home went off, turning the house completely dark.

"Not this shit again!" Jarvis exclaimed in the dark. "They just fixed the power a couple days . . . !"

Boom!

"What the fuck?" he exclaimed frantically as he dove to the floor at the sound of his front door being rammed down. He immediately reached for his two Glock .19s under his Polo shirt and rapidly squeezed off at the intruders.

Boc! Boc! Boc!

The shots ricocheted off of the FBI shield.

When Jarvis saw the flashlights, it dawned on him that he was shooting at unannounced authorities, until they spoke.

"FBI. Please cease your fire and lay down your weapons!" Agent Clemons ordered as she then threw a flash bang grenade toward Jarvis's location.

Bang!

When Jarvis's eyes caught the flash, he immediately dropped his smoking weapons and reached for his blinded eyes.

"FBI! Lay down now!" Clemons screamed as she made a dash toward Jarvis with her Glock .21 and flashlight aimed in a defensive stance.

Behind her was her partner, Agent Norton, who was ready to make Jarvis's day red. But unfortunately, Clemons was running the show, and she was less impassive to the bad guys. If it was left to Norton, Jarvis would've been a dead man; instead, he was cuffing him behind his back, taking him into custody instead of taking him to the morgue.

"Mr. Poole . . . we meet again," Agent Norton said as he roughly secured the cuffs on Jarvis.

"1209 . . . please return power to 2132 Pine Road," Clemons spoke to the power workers down the road into her walkie-talkie.

"Ten-four."

Less than a minute later, all the lights came back on in the mansion, illuminating the excessive shells and bullet-wrecked walls caused by Jarvis.

"Someone needs better practice with their shooting," Clemons joked. "Someone grab the guns and run them to see if they're clean," she ordered her fellow officers, who immediately grabbed Jarvis's weapons off the ground and tossed them into plastic bags.

"Jarvis . . . tell me . . . where is Champagne, huh? Where is your girlfriend?" Clemons asked Jarvis, who was still unable to see from the effects of the grenade.

Damn! Jarvis thought at the mention of his baby's name.

"Talk, Jarvis. Is she here . . . ?"

"There's no one here, Clemons. We've searched thoroughly. If she's here, she's not alive," a backup officer stated breathlessly from rummaging through the mansion.

"So, where is she, Jarvis?" Norton asked.

"I don't know who y'all talking about!" he responded.

"Oh, really?" Clemons retorted, with a smile on her face.

Just what I need to hear, Clemons thought.

* * *

Shaquana sat on the leather sofa eating the last of her fried chicken and hot sauce while watching the AMBER alert on the news about her best friend. When the front door opened to the suite and she saw Maurice, she placed her plate of chicken bones down and ran into his warming arms.

"Baby, I'm scared!" she said as she buried her head in his chest.

"Don't be, baby! Everything will be fine. Never expected the worst!" he said to her while soothing her curls on her head.

Despite him still being hurt by her creeping around on him and lying to him when he proved her integrity, Maurice was concerned about his woman, knowing her state of mind could be affected by being so worried.

"Baby, I'm here, and you need not let negative thoughts invade your mind," he said.

"It's been two months of not hearing from her . . . it's not like Champagne," Shaquana said, wiping away the cascading tears from her face with the sleeve of her Gucci sweater.

"Listen to me!" Maurice said as he lifted her chin and stared into her watery eyes.

Damn! he thought, hating to see her the way she was, all torn apart mentally and destroyed emotionally.

"Let's not worry ourselves. Maybe she's on her own vacation, getting away from the world after what happen . . . !"

"What about Jarvis? Do you think he left her and made her run mad?" she asked him.

"We don't know nobody else's problems, especially when we have our own . . ."

"What problems do we have, Maurice?" she asked him skeptically.

Did he know about Kenneth? Damn! It's not like I'm cheating on him. I'm just not ready to let him know I have a male friend, Shaquana thought as her eyes betrayed her thoughts.

Yeah! Let's not act brand new about your little fling with Ken, Maurice thought angrily as he then pulled away from Shaquana and walked to the kitchen.

"Maurice . . . what's wrong with you?" Shaquana asked him as he rummaged through the refrigerator for an almost empty jug of orange juice.

"Damn it, Shaquana! When was the last time you went grocery shopping . . . ?"

Oh, let me be reminded . . . fast-food joints is your take these days, Maurice thought as he slammed the refrigerator door vigorously.

He knew that Shaquana had been spending plenty of time with Ken, because he had been watching them for the last two weeks drive to school together and have lunch together during their breaks.

"Maurice . . . I'm sorry, baby. I'll go tomorrow . . ."

"Don't worry about it, Shaquana. Just start bringing me a meal or two from the Chinese joint next time . . ."

What the fuck! He knows! Damn! she realized as she stood speechless and watched Maurice storm from the suite.

She didn't want to jump to any conclusions or accept the coincidental remark, but she played it cool.

"Maurice, baby . . . where are you going?" she screamed while running behind him with her heart beating rapidly.

When he was out the door in the hallway, Maurice turned around with a feigned smile on his face and said, "I'm hungry, so I'm gonna get me some Chinese food. What . . . you thought I was playing? Are you coming or staying?"

Don't go girl! her conscience shouted out to her, but she refused to listen to her gut.

"Yeah, wait up. I don't want to go in my pajamas."

"I'll be in the car. Hurry up!" Maurice retorted and then went outside.

* * *

It wasn't until Shaquana and Maurice had traveled a mile into the midnight atmosphere that she realized that there could be no possible Chinese joint open at such a late hour. This revelation left her bothered.

Why do I feel like I'm doing something wrong? she thought while vaguely listening to Drake's hit emanate from Maurice's surround sound.

"I know when that highlight bling . . . that could only mean one thing!" Maurice sang to the lyrics.

Tell him, girl, and stop being afraid of his reaction! her conscience encouragingly shouted out to her.

But she couldn't muster the strength or audacity to tell him.

"Wonder if she out there bending over backward for someone else?" Maurice continued to intentionally serenade

Drake's lyrics to Shaquana, who indeed caught the conveying curveball.

Not being able to take it any longer, she reached over and turned down the volume to Drake's hit.

Don't jump to conclusions! she thought, vagrantly searching for the right words to explain Kenneth, but she couldn't.

Instead, she was afraid and nonchalantly blurted out, "You love that song, huh? Well, that shit is so played out, Maurice. I hear it every day."

Shaquana looked over at Maurice with a pout on her face, to which he looked over at her as if she were some creature.

Bitch! You don't think creeping played out? Maurice wanted to know.

He couldn't explain why he wasn't ready to confront her with her infidelity. There was no doubt that he had evidence—and a damaged heart. But he was different from the ordinary man who would have exploded.

There's a time for everything. A time to be peaceful and a time to be corrupted . . . most definitely there is! he thought.

"Maurice . . . why have you been staying out late lately?" She found a bone to pick.

"Busy! You know how that goes," he retorted nonchalantly.

"Really? So we dry talking now, Maurice?" Shaquana said as she slid over to him and immersed below the dashboard while unfastening the belt to his black jeans.

Please him, girl! her conscience suggested.

"What are you doing? Back up!" Maurice said, pushing her away with his free hand while swerving in traffic.

Damn! she thought of his rejection.

"So, you really going to tell me that I can't suck my man's dick?" Shaquana inquired with a pout.

Bitch! Suck Ken's dick! Maurice thought angrily.

"I'm not feeling it."

"Did I do something to . . . ?"

When Maurice pulled into Peacocks restaurant where she and Kenneth ate lunch together every day and talked about their careers, Shaquana became speechless, and her heart began to race.

"What's the matter? You act like you've seen a ghost, baby," Maurice said as he noticed the surprised look on her face.

Yeah, bitch! Maurice don't miss shit—nothing! he thought.

"Maurice . . . it's midnight. Where the fuck is you going to find an open Chinese restaurant? This place is closed!" Shaquana said, bridling her panicked consciousness.

Damn! She good . . . and dangerous! Maurice thought.

"I forgot. Damn! Maybe we could find us something to eat at Wendy's. I hate that it's closed. I hear that their lunch is delicious . . ."

He knows! Shaquana thought.

"Have you ever tried their lunch, baby?" he asked her.

Shaquana's time to tell him about her friend, Ken, was now; instead, she said, "No! Let's go to Taco Bell. This place is closed."

Twelve

"So we're going to play these games, Mr. Poole? How far do you plan on getting, huh?"

Agent Clemons and her boss, FBI Director Bernie Scott, both were listening to Norton interrogate Jarvis for hours now behind the mirror-tinted window.

"Like I said, let me see my lawyer," Jarvis insisted.

"He's a fucking jackass!" Clemons said to her boss.

"Sooner or later, he'll get the picture that we are his lawyers until he breaks," Scott said to Clemons, who was his favorite, and soon-to-be lieutenant, unbeknownst to her.

Bernie Scott was a tall, lanky, gray-haired veteran of the FBI, who was in his late sixties. He was still adamant about not giving the force up anytime soon, and he believed to have it in him until age ninety. Everyone on the force loved him because he was fair and compassionate to his employees.

"What's up with the phone . . . ?"

"Robinson or that jackass?" Clemons asked Scott.

"Robinson!" he retorted while taking a sip of his steaming hot cup of Maxwell House coffee.

"Her phone was found in his bedroom. It was dead, but we've booted it and retrieved all the data from it. Her last call was to Shaquana Clark, and like she stated, Champagne's phone shut off and there was no more connection between them."

"So, this girl just disappeared—poof!" Scott said with emphasis.

"That's what it looks like," Clemons answered.

"Go in and play the good, pretty cop you are," Scott directed Clemons while texting Norton and informing him to back out.

Scott and Clemons watched Norton reach into his slacks, remove his iPhone, and read the message.

"I'ma give you some time to think about the hole you're climbing into, Poole. Please make the smart decision and tell us where to find Champagne's body at least," Norton said as he stormed out of the room.

A moment later, Norton appeared behind the mirror-tinted glass with Clemons and Director Scott.

"He's a jackass! I swear I want to nail him!" Norton said as he watched the calm, expressionless Jarvis sit at the table in the interrogation room.

"He's definitely cold-blooded," Clemons retorted. "Well, I guess it's my turn," she continued as she walked out of the room and appeared in the interrogation room a moment later.

"Hello, Jarvis. Umm . . . do you need anything to drink or eat?" she asked in a seductive voice.

"She's good," Scott said.

"I want my lawyer," Jarvis insisted.

"Listen, Jarvis . . . your lawyer can't help you now. Only you can!" Clemons said, pointing at him as she sat close to him on the table.

Her suit was extremely tight-fitting and accentuated her delicate curves, but Jarvis wasn't moved by the tricks of beauty.

"These people have people talking, Jarvis. They know about Benjamin's murder and who all were involved. How do you think we know all this stuff, huh?" Clemons asked while Jarvis remained quiet but not too naive not to be digesting what she was saying.

Jarvis was a veteran to interrogations, and it was Benjamin who taught him to remain calm and quiet and keep on asking for some type of representation.

"Big Funk and Corey have already spilled the beans, so sooner or later you or your lawyer will have to give these people an explanation . . . so stop being stupid!" Clemons suggested as she moved in closer to Jarvis, violating his air space and causing him to back away.

Bitch thinking that seducing shit works. Bitch! How about reading The Art of Seduction, he thought to himself.

"They know all the players in Benjamin Clark's death and will make someone pay for it. Despite the authorities' ill-will toward the man, their job is to get justice by all means," Clemons said.

Somebody's talking . . . that I know. But they obviously still don't have no proof because these motherfuckers are fishing hard! Jarvis contemplated.

"Jarvis . . . who is Tameka?"

Yeah, someone's talking! he thought.

"Did you see that?" Scott asked Norton.

At the mention of Tameka's name, Jarvis's demeanor fluctuated from calm to a slight flinch and break out of perspiration.

"I saw exactly what you saw, boss," Norton retorted.

"Go in there and press Tameka's role until we have a perfect picture of her. Whoever she is, she seems dangerous!" Scott said.

"Looks like we have our first break in Poole," Norton suggested.

"Go get 'em, tiger!" Scott retorted as Norton left to assist Clemons.

* * *

Daquan walked into the lawyer-client room and saw Arlene sitting at a round table. She looked as beautiful as always. Despite being happy to see her, Daquan wasn't expecting to see her by herself when he was summoned to report for his lawyer's visit.

"Where's Goodman?" Daquan asked Arlene while pulling his seat in to the table.

"Damn, someone's not happy to see me, huh?" Arlene retorted, with a gorgeous hypnotizing smile that made Daquan's manhood do flips.

Damn! She's bad! he thought.

"Nah! It's nothing like that! It's just I at least expected to see Goodman here as well," Daquan said nervously, for she was causing him to extremely blush on the inside.

"Well, Mr. Goodman is in court today handling a trial at the moment. And he wanted me to get over here to inform you of the status of your case. Umm . . . ," she said while tapping her designed nails on the table, "soon, we will be moving to present to the court a motion to suppress evidence . . ."

"What else would be suppressed?" Daquan asked, surprising Arlene, for she thought he was ingenuous to the law and wouldn't know anything about legal procedures.

But obviously he does. This kid knows his stuff, Arlene thought.

Daquan had turned sixteen since being incarcerated, and he had more wisdom and understanding of the law than a lot of old-head and old-school convicts in the Jonesboro jail.

"So, I see you understand the legal procedures well, Daquan. That's good!" Arlene exclaimed effusively.

"Well, I have to be aware of what is going on around me. Can't let y'all do all the work," Daquan joked.

"Well, to answer your question . . . we're moving to get the gun suppressed on grounds that it was illegally obtained. We're also trying to remove Shay Graham's statement she made
to . . ."

"She's dead. How could they use it?" Daquan asked curiously.

"Correct, but if we don't move to strike it, then we're allowing them to bring it in freely. We don't want the jury to hear any statements from a dead witness—period!" Arlene explained.

She's right, he thought.

"Everything is going to be okay, Daquan . . ."

"So, when do we go?" he asked, cutting her off, eager to get inside the courtroom to be set free.

Because these bitches don't have no case, he thought.

"We will move for a pretrial motion in thirty days, okay?" she said cheerfully.

"Okay. Thanks for everything," Daquan told her.

"You're welcome," she said while standing.

Damn! Daquan thought while mesmerized by her sexy frame that was accentuated well through her cotton-elastane dress.

"Umm . . . have a nice day, Arlene," he said.

"You, too. And remember . . . don't discuss your case with no one, because there is no one to trust," she said, pointing her finger at Daquan.

She then walked away with loud clanking leather strap heels as Daquan watched her walk through the exit door and got a full view of her ghetto-fabulous ass.

Damn! She bad! he thought.

Daquan was so caught up in his lust and Arlene's beauty that he missed the most intrinsic advice. Had he paid attention and taken heed, it might have saved him from his enemies surrounding him that he couldn't see through the deception and many masks that they wore.

* * *

Tameka was back in Miami relaxing in her Jacuzzi after having a long, intense round of sex with D-Zoe. She then sent him on his way, so she could become saturated in her peace of mind. After having dinner with Cuban Black, he had invited her back to his hotel suite, something that turned out to be torturous for her as she refrained from raping him. The man was a real gentleman in all aspects, and she was seriously digging his swagger.

Just the smell of him aroused her sexual operations. By the time she left his suite, her satin panties were soaked in her woman juices, and she had no choice but to go back to her hotel and masturbate into exhaustion.

When Tameka made it back to Miami, she literally attacked D-Zoe in the back of the limo and fucked him good and hard, never caring about the company up front hearing her cries of pleasure. When they made it to their beach house, it restarted, from the kitchen to the bedroom. The saddest part of the hard-core roller coaster was that instead of D-Zoe, every stroke and electrifying touch she imagined was by Cuban Black. She wanted him to make her speak his language, never minding his wives. She was only concerned with a good fuck.

Tameka would never make the mistake of commitment to a man again. Not after her ex and his abusiveness, as well as Jarvis and his deception. She would never let another man get close to her again. There would always be an expedient purpose with whomever she chose to lay down with.

Sitting in the Jacuzzi, Tameka was now thinking about her and D-Zoe's fling.

He is getting too close . . . and taking his feelings seriously. Something that I can't have, she thought.

It didn't matter how many times she had sat him down and explained that it would do him no good to think what they had going could get serious. She was always blunt with him about her only interest in him, which was for him to push her cocaine throughout Little Haiti to Palm Beach and fuck her good when she needed it. But she saw that D-Zoe wasn't built to carry out her expectations. He blew up her phone the entire time she was in Georgia, to the point that she had to turn it off and ignore his sweet texts.

"He was getting out of hand," Tameka said as she took a sip of her coconut Cîroc.

I know the look of love, and I can't have that. He was ready to jump on Jean for a pussy that wasn't his, she thought, shaking her head in disappointment.

"Damn it, D-Zoe! I got to cut it off with you or at least slow down," Tameka said.

Her thoughts then fluctuated to Jarvis, and she smiled.

"I will make sure you get me my half billion, and then I'll take your damn life for hurting me, bitch-ass nigga! You'll never shit on this Palm Beach woman again!" she cried out, with tears cascading down her face from the pain that Jarvis had caused her.

She had run away from her family and abusive boyfriend, just to run into another tragedy—one that seemed to leave a permanent scar on her heart. There was nothing to bring Benjamin back—but death to the one who had stolen life from her and Benjamin.

Cuban Black had made her his second-in-command and general over the Haitians. Her calls were her calls, and it was her duty to control the streets while he stayed legit and remained a low-key profile.

The streets in Miami were hers, and she had sent D-Zoe and K-Zoe to wipe out every establishment that Haitian Beny had, for she wanted no one who dealt with him like family under Cuban Black.

Miami is about to bleed tonight, because a new bitch is in town . . . "The Diva of the South!" Tameka thought.

* * *

Coco had all the niggas in King of Diamond breaking their necks at her lustrous swaying hips and succulent ass that jiggled in her mini silk dress. She walked toward the bar ignoring all the ballers' calls to hold their attention, with her mind and eye on one individual. The exotic dancers had nothing on her, and she knew that beyond any dubious thoughts, she was indeed the eye candy of the night, and envious hos were all tuned in while her eye candy sat in VIP doing it big. It was his birthday, and she had every means of making his night one to outdo any other birthday he had ever had.

His name was Tankhead, and he was a flashy Haitian from Little Haiti, who everyone knew well. When it came to the meanest hustler in Little Haiti, it was him, for he was the third chairman in the Zo'pound gang. He tricked away large sums of cash every night between the strip clubs and local clubs. He was jet black, stood five eight, weighed 195 pounds, and was uglier than could be described. He was a notorious yet well-respected iron slanger. Coco ordered herself a bottle of Hennessy and strutted over to the VIP. When she got to the ropes, the bouncer looked at her like she had shit on her face and not like she was the baddest bitch among them all.

"Excuse me, but I don't see no VIP band on your wrist, lil mama!" the six five bouncer named Buna said.

"Maybe I don't need one!" she retorted loudly over the Lil Wayne hit serenading the ecstatic club.

The nigga looked at her and laughed like she was some type of comedian. "Baby . . . you could go down to 151st and stand up and get a bigger laugh than mine!" he screamed.

"Just like I thought. You'll act like a ho, nigga," she said to the bouncer, whose face formed into a frown.

"Bitch! What did you say?" he asked, getting up in her grill.

"You heard me. Come down to my level and see!" Coco said while backing up and simultaneously lifting up the front of her dress, showing the bouncer her nicely shaven pussy.

"More pussy than you got nuts, nigga!" Coco retorted.

Damn! This bitch is fine and got a fat-ass pussy, Buna thought. *Slap that ho. She's disrespecting this nigga*, his conscience told him.

"So, what's that mean?"

"It mean let her through," a voice said from behind the bouncer.

When he turned around, he was looking into the eyes of Tankhead.

"Good job, Buna. She's with me. She means no harm!" he said while locking eyes with Coco. "Ain't that right, baby girl?"

"Yes, daddy! I just want to celebrate your big night proper. I promise to behave the entire night, daddy!" Coco said seductively while walking up to Tankhead and embracing him.

Damn, this ugly-ass nigga got them hos going crazy! Buna thought.

* * *

"Damn, daddy. That tongue good. Eat this pussy, nigga!" Coco purred as Tankhead ate her pussy in the backseat of his limo. His head was buried in her mound, flicking his tongue across her clitoris like he was eating a juicy watermelon. Her dress was pulled up to her stomach, exposing her flawless pecan tone.

With her hands on the back of his head, she gyrated her hips while pumping her mound in his face. A Pretty Ricky song blared from the speakers, putting them both in the mood. He wanted badly to fuck her, but she told him to save the pound game for the hotel room and then demanded he eat her pussy and make her cum before they went there.

Coco had made Tankhead abandon all of his hoochie mamas who thought they were going to be his entertainment for the night. She was killing his entire entourage, and Tankhead quickly let it be known that he had found his match for tonight, and he had no interest in any other bitches.

They were on their way to a mid-class hotel out in the city to remain low-key so that no one would spot Coco with an estranged man. For she told him in so many words that she was the wife of Cuban Black, walking in disguise, and that they were going through their ups-and-downs stage at the moment. It wasn't hard for Tankhead to make his grave mistake, despite working for Haitian Beny, who was believed to be connected to Cuban Black. Pussy had its own value to it, and niggas were dying from it every day.

Damn! This ugly-ass nigga knows that he can work that tongue, she thought.

"Oh shit! I'm cumming!" she purred as her load came down and was slurped up by Tankhead.

He cleaned her good with his tongue before he came up for a breath.

Her pussy was like water—odorless, Tankhead thought as he cracked open the sunroof for some air.

"So are you feeling okay, birthday boy?" Coco asked while cuddling up with Tankhead in his genuine embrace.

"Of course, baby girl. I want this night to last a lifetime . . ."

"Nigga, kill that! I told you I'm married. Don't get out of control. Maybe we need to just skip the pounding part if you're going to act all sprung out!"

"Then that mean we might as well handle it now if we planning on skipping it at the 'tel," Tankhead said.

"I'm just saying," she said, poking Tankhead in the face friskily. "Don't get caught up, daddy!"

"I won't, baby. I promise. Okay?" he said as the limo pulled up to a Holiday Inn.

"We're here, baby girl. Let me go handle the fee," Tankhead told her, pulling out a hefty wad of cash from his fitted jeans, being flashy as always.

"Okay, baby," she retorted.

When the limo halted under the porte cochere in front of the lobby, a black SUV pulled up behind with its lights still on. Neither Tankhead nor his driver sensed anything amiss, only expecting it to be another hotel guest.

"Hurry, daddy! Because my pussy crying to be pounded!" Coco said while rubbing on Tankhead's bulging dick through his jeans.

"Hold that thought!" he suggested as he stepped out of the limo. Before he had time to close the door, a deadly fusillade took him by surprise.

Boc! Boc! Boc! Boc! Boc!

The shots entered his chest, head, and neck, and dropped him to his death.

The loud gunshots and Coco's screams could be heard throughout the hotel.

When the limo driver stepped out to join the gunfight, he let a Mac-10 spit rapidly at the assassins in the SUV, and he too was brought down by their deadly fusillade.

Still screaming, Coco saw a masked assassin rush up to her with his weapon drawn at her.

"Bitch! Let's go!" he said, pulling her by her curly locks and pressing his weapon to her head. He speed-walked her to the SUV and tossed her in the backseat, climbing in with her.

When the door closed, K-Zoe kissed his woman deeply and passionately as D-Zoe accelerated from the scene.

Thirteen

The news about Tankhead's murder was the talk of all the hoods in Miami, and the Zo'pound gang was furious and out looking for those who were responsible for one of their leader's deaths. But like the authorities, the streets were far from learning that the three people involved were relaxing at Tameka's beach house on South Beach, and that their new boos were the ones who'd actually sent the hit.

Coco and Tameka wore identical sexy satin bikinis, while D-Zoe and K-Zoe relaxed in Polo swim shorts, smoking kush and drinking Hennessy on the rocks. Coco and Tameka sipped from their martinis as they sat at the edge of the back wooden patio in their beach chairs. From the inside surround system, Trina emanated loudly, which put both women in their grooves.

"Meka . . . you should have seen that nigga face when I told him that I was Cuban Black's wife. He didn't give a fuck about nothing," Coco said sluggishly, from slamming back two martinis back to back.

Unbeknownst to Tameka, last night had scared Coco to death, despite knowing beforehand how things were going to play out. She just wasn't accustomed to murder yet. Even after seeing Big Dee get killed, she kept her poker face on, but she still felt a bit odd. She knew that Tameka was a ruthless woman, and Coco played her close, with feigned excitement from her bloodshed.

"One thing about these niggas, Coco, is that no matter what and how much you've treated them good, they will still cut-throat themselves," Tameka exclaimed, getting the attention of D-Zoe who had heard her over K-Zoe conversing with him about sports. They were both standing by the ramp, out of earshot, while they smoked their kush.

"So, how are you and K-Zoe, Coco?" Tameka asked.

"He's okay. We're hitting it hard!" Coco exclaimed, smiling and blushing. "Praying that I ain't gotta kill one of these Miami bitches and his slick ass," Coco retorted.

"Girl, you are blushing like a motherfucker! I know he rocking your world," Tameka said ecstatically.

"Exactly!" she retorted.

When Tameka looked over at D-Zoe and K-Zoe, she locked eyes with K-Zoe, and then she looked at D-Zoe, whose eyes were on her too.

Damn! I could take both of them if I wanted to, but I already know how D-Zoe would act, Tameka thought, imagining how it would feel to have K-Zoe in the bedroom as well.

She didn't care that K-Zoe was her homegirl's man.

Shit! Many men and women crossed the line. And what a bitch doesn't know won't hurt her, Tameka thought as she turned her head away from the two handsome Haitians.

"So tomorrow would you be available and sober to carry out this next mission that I need done?" Tameka asked Coco.

Damn! This bitch never stops! Coco thought before answering.

"Of course. Just let me sleep these martinis off, gal, and I'll be as good as new."

"That's great, Coco. I really appreciate you," Tameka said sincerely.

"D-Zoe . . . could you please go pick up the mail for me at the second PO box. I'm looking for an important letter that should be there," she asked him.

"Yeah, baby. I'll get on that right away . . ."

"And please stop by the store and grab a gallon of Seagram's gin, will you? And don't forget the cranberry juice, honey!" Tameka ordered D-Zoe, who was already sliding into a black wifebeater.

"I will handle everything, baby . . ."

"Nigga, stop with that baby shit!" Tameka exploded.

"Sorry, Meka. It . . ."

"Don't need to explain. We've talked about this, D-Zoe," she retorted, reminding him that they were only fuck friends and not a couple. She was his boss and not his bitch.

Coco looked over at Tameka and then at K-Zoe, who was surprised to see how Tameka had D-Zoe's head gone. K-Zoe had never seen his boy so submissive and obsessed with a woman that would never love him like he loved her.

They say pussy has power! K-Zoe thought.

"I'll be back, Meka," D-Zoe said as he stormed off.

Well, I'll be damned! Coco thought as she lay back in her beach chair and closed her eyes.

K-Zoe stood by himself now, leaning against the wooden rail to the walkway down to the beach. When he looked up, he once again locked eyes with Tameka, who boldly stared him down seductively. K-Zoe knew that it was a look of lust in her eyes, and the dog came out of him. He pulled his erect love tool out and stroked himself twice. The sight of his enormous chocolate tool aroused her sexual desire and made her wet between her legs. Tameka looked over at Coco and saw that she had dozed off.

Go get that dick, girl! her conscience screamed out to her. She stood up slowly and crept off discreetly, trying not to awaken Coco. As she walked through the sliding doors into the beach house, K-Zoe tucked himself in and followed her inside.

* * *

D-Zoe didn't appreciate how Tameka had talked to him in front of his homeboy and his bitch, especially exposing their stipulations in their relationship.

"It's okay, baby. You'll break out of that shit as long as I continue to fuck your ass like it's mine. You'll catch the flow, baby gal!" D-Zoe said as he pulled his conspicuous Chevy Caprice inside the crowded post office parking lot.

When he stepped out of the car, he thought about paying one of his play toys a visit. Last time he saw his friend and explored her world, he almost said fuck Tameka and sailed off with his forbidden fruit.

Now that bitch pussy had Tameka shit on the door! D-Zoe thought as he walked inside the crowded post office.

* * *

"What the fuck!"

Smack!

Coco yelled out, jumping out of her sleep while slapping her thigh and killing the red ant that had bitten her.

When Coco looked around, she saw that she was alone.

"Damn! Where the fuck is everybody? I know these bitches ain't leave me out here!" she said sluggishly.

She scanned the beach and saw no one in the water but the neighbors.

"Damn! I got to fucking pee!" she said hastily, moving to hurry to the restroom, expecting to find everyone inside.

How long was I asleep? she thought as she walked through the sliding back door and saw no one in the kitchen or living room.

As she quickly took the stairs in a hurry to the restroom, she heard the irrefutable sounds of Tameka's moans.

Damn, D-Zoe. She was just blowing your ass off, and now she crying for mercy, Coco thought, smiling.

As she neared the stairs, Tameka's moans intensified, and Coco saw that the door to her room was open. She bent a right and headed to the restroom, but stopped in her tracks when she heard Tameka scream out: "K-Zoe! Shit!"

Coco stood frozen in her tracks in shock as she tried to register what she'd just heard.

Maybe I got D-Zoe mixed up with K-Zoe, she thought.

But that thought proved to be wrong when she heard her man's voice, which could never be mistaken for D-Zoe's.

* * *

"You like this dick, bitch, huh?" K-Zoe said as he fucked Tameka hard from the back and slapped her on her ass.

Smack!

"Yes, K-Zoe. Yes!" Tameka moaned out loud while ramming backward into K-Zoe's strokes.

Damn, this nigga could fuck a bitch world up! she thought as she felt K-Zoe's dick in her stomach.

"Uhhh! Uhhh! Shit!" she moaned out, choking on her sobs.

K-Zoe couldn't see the tears on her face cascading. Tameka knew that D-Zoe was now out of the picture, because he never made her cry. She had no understanding of why she was crying, for it was ineffable. All she knew was that K-Zoe had triggered something that no other man had before.

"I'm cumming!" she screamed, trembling and climaxing strongly.

"Arrgghhh! Shit, bitch!" K-Zoe groaned as he pulled out and shot his load on Tameka's caramel ass cheeks and back.

Neither of them sensed Coco standing in the doorway with a flood of tears streaming down her face.

Coco quickly stormed away from the heartbreaking revelation and pissed herself as she returned back outside.

This bitch is cold, and I will show the two of them! Coco thought as she left the beach house on foot with her towel and purse.

She hailed a taxi down the road and returned to her and K-Zoe's place.

Fourteen

S haquana didn't have to be in school until 10:00 a.m., and it was just hitting 8:15. She decided to visit her little brother in jail for an hour and then meet Ken for breakfast at IHOP in College Park before they reported to class.

As she waited for Daquan, Shaquana thought about her and Kenneth's friendship. He was a male friend, which she never had in her life besides her dad—and growing up and seeing Jarvis as a brother and crush. Kenneth had finally convinced her to follow him once school was over and take the same law enforcement route as him. He was eager to join the DEA.

And he has every means of going after the ones putting the drugs on the streets . . . including my man, Shaquana thought.

Kenneth often told her about the potential she had to be the detective she wanted to become, and he promised her that he would help her find her parents' killers.

Since Maurice's last stunt of taking her to Peacock's restaurant at an extremely late hour, Shaquana had switched to another restaurant to avoid running into him. In her gut, she felt that he knew her every move, but when she went to look for him, he was never there. She loved Maurice, and despite knowing that Ken had a thing for her, she would not cheat on her man. Kenneth respected her and Maurice's relationship and never went further than reminding her how gorgeous she was. He left his baby mama and was a handsome, single man, who was focused more on his career than seeking a new love. But there were still a lot of stones that hadn't been turned over about Kenneth.

Shaquana was far from knowing that Kenneth was waiting patiently for her and planning to bring down her man. She was too blinded by his tactical cleverness to foresee his true intentions, and she was too deep to change the foreordained results.

When she saw Daquan appear, she smiled at her brother and took notice of his weight gain.

"Damn, nigga! You looking a little chubby there!" she said, laughing.

"Yeah, I'm steady putting on, sis. What's up? How is everything besides Champagne running away?"

"She's still missing . . . no trace, brah!" she said sadly.

"I hear they have Jarvis."

"Yeah, they do. But obviously they don't have enough evidence, because he's not charged with nothing. And . . . ," she said and then sighed, "detectives are investigating him in Dad's murder."

"Tell me you're lying, Sis!" Daquan said, with a surge of emotion, and tears forming in the wells of his eyes.

It badly hurt Shaquana to see her brother hurt, and she knew how much he loved his father, no different than she did.

"Yes, Brother. He's being investigated . . ."

"Tell Mauri to come see me, Sis, please!" Daquan begged.

I'll be damned. I let these crackers get him. Suspicion is all I needed, Daquan thought as the irresistible tears finally fell from his eyes.

"Okay, Daquan. I will tell him to come," Shaquana said.

* * *

Walking out the front door of the jail, Shaquana let out a long, stress-filled sigh as she hastened to her car. She hated seeing Daquan hurt, and she had no clue of why Maurice's visit was so important for him. He begged her with tears in the wells of his eyes.

"Whatever he wanted Maurice for . . . isn't good," she mumbled. "And it isn't my business," she retorted as she made it to her car.

Once inside, she pulled out her iPhone and called Kenneth, who was listed as "Teacher" in her contacts. *Why am I hiding this man like we are creeping? I need . . . she considered.*

"What's up, beautiful?" Ken said, interrupting her thoughts.

Shaquana smiled, for she loved the way he called her sweet names.

"Good morning, Ken. What are you doing?" she asked.

"Doing the same thing you're doing," he retorted. "Heading over to IHOP. What . . . you forget?" Ken asked her, knowing that it would be the first thing on her mind and last to forget.

"No, I'm on my way. See you there," she said before she hung up the phone.

She sat a moment before starting her car. As she navigated out of the jail's district and hopped on the interstate to College Park, she attempted to call Maurice but got no answer.

"Fuck!" she exclaimed angrily, tossing her phone onto the passenger seat and accelerating ten miles over the required speed limit. For some reason, she was eager to see Kenneth—like always. He was just a friend, she thought, unaware of the black Charger trailing her.

* * *

"So, you're telling me that Tameka is the ex-girlfriend of Benjamin and Jarvis . . . and Benjamin is the one who killed Tameka's boyfriend who was found slain in the apartment?" Agent Norton asked Big Funk for the umpteenth time in three hours.

"Yes, that's correct. Like I told you, sir . . . I have no reason to lie . . ."

"We're not saying that you are, Lewis. We just want to make sure that we're all on the same page," Agent Clemons explained to him.

Big Funk rubbed the stress and perspiration from his face with his massive hands and then let out a long sigh.

"What is Corey telling you guys?" Big Funk asked.

"He's telling us exactly the same thing, Lewis. He wants to take his ten years like a badge of honor. I can say that for certain," Norton replied.

"I'm telling you guys, it's true. If he goes to trial, I will sit down on the stand, okay," Big Funk said, stressed.

"Good job, Funk. That's all our concern is," Norton said.

"So where do we find Tameka?" Clemons asked.

"Last I knew, she went to Miami and joined Haitian Beny's force to bring down Jarvis for how he beat her to sleep at the club," Big Funk admitted.

"And she's behind Big Dee's murder at the club?" Clemons asked.

Big Funk looked at Clemons for a moment in silence, and looked beyond her beauty. He knew that Clemons knew the answers before she asked, and he saw how much of a pit bull in a skirt she was. He had nothing to lose by telling her the truth. He had already told them everything repeatedly in the last couple weeks after agreeing to ten years in federal prison.

"Agent Clemons," Big Funk began before taking a long pause, "this woman has proved to be a dangerous person, and it all starts with her beauty. It got her ex-boyfriend slain in her apartment, it got Benjamin killed, and give it enough time, and it will get Jarvis killed. She's not just behind Big Dee's murder, the woman is the boss who instructed him to die," Big Funk said, pumping the FBI with reliable information.

"So tell me," Clemons said when she thought of a prospect, "do you believe that Tameka may be behind Champagne's disappearance?"

"If I could bet that she was, then I'd win that bet!" Big Funk said with a smile on his face.

Both Norton and Clemons looked at each other and realized that their bait needed to be set free in order to test the waters. The look in their eyes explained that they were on the same page. And as if on cue, both agents spoke together.

"Thank . . ."

"Sorry!" Clemons said.

"No, go ahead," Norton retorted.

"Thank you, Mr. Lewis. We will be in touch."

* * *

"What's up now, pussy-ass cracker?" Earl exclaimed as he was being pulled over by a state trooper.

He was on his way to his mom's place to check up on her and take her out to eat, where he planned to surprise her with the good news that he soon would be a father, and she'd be a grandmother. He did not need to be face-to-face with some tobacco-chewing, redneck ass, for his patience was slim. Earl waited patiently for the officer to walk up to his driver's side window while his car was still running.

Tap! Tap! Tap!

I know this cracker is not beating on my shit with that damn nightstick like he crazy, Earl thought as he slid down his window.

"Excuse me, sir, but where do they say in the law that an officer during a traffic stop has the right to damage the paint on my shit?" Earl asked sternly.

As expected, the officer was indeed a redneck with a mouthful of tobacco and looked at Earl like he'd lost his mind.

"So, you're one of the smart niggas, huh?" the officer said, spitting tobacco juice onto Earl's 30-inch rims.

"Cracker! Since you want to call me a nigger, how 'bout you turn the camera on and say them same words . . ."

"Are you threatening me, boy?" the officer screamed as two more troopers pulled up behind his car unbeknownst to Earl, who never saw one of the troopers walking up to his passenger side window.

"Boy! Cracker! Where did you go to school to disrespect a man like me, huh?" Earl asked, reaching to unfasten his seat belt while staring into the redneck officer's eyes.

I'm a beat this cracker ass! Earl thought as he fumbled to find the button.

Earl's movements were mistaken for him reaching for a gun, and the officer on the passenger side pulled his weapon and repeatedly fired inside the SUV, hitting Earl in his head. The officer shot from the back and worked his way to the passenger window, filling Earl's body with an excessive count of bullets from his Glock .21. Earl was dead from the first shot—after only reaching to unfasten his seatbelt.

"Suspect use of force administered, and actions ceased immediately . . . suspect is unresponsive, and officer is unharmed," the officer who just killed Earl said into his radio.

He then smiled at his fellow redneck officer.

"Damn, George! Looks like Carl's ahead of you now!" the third policeman said to the officer who pulled over Earl for a DWB (driving while black).

"Don't worry! I'll have one before the end of the week," George said determinedly.

* * *

"Jarvis Poole . . . pack your property. You're being released," the female guard explained over the speaker.

He was locked down in the hole after disrespecting a female sergeant when he was being processed in booking on probable cause.

Apparently the motherfuckers couldn't charge me! he thought as he got all his property, which was nothing more than what he could carry in his bare hands.

Being that the police never announced themselves when kicking down his door, Jarvis had the right to fire his weapon, for he was under the impression that they were robbers and not FBI agents. He respected their honesty, because they could have easily lied and stated that on arrival they had announced themselves.

But they didn't, Jarvis thought.

"Are you ready to go, Mr. Poole?" the lady on the intercom asked.

"I'm ready to go get me some pussy . . . yeah!" Jarvis retorted sincerely.

His baby was somewhere being held captive, and he was alone . . . until he rescued her.

I think I'ma take me a trip to Jacksonville and smell the Florida atmosphere and taste their pussy vine, Jarvis thought eagerly.

Fifteen

The news of Earl's death was everywhere and had Jonesboro once again in a state of grief. Brenda was completely damaged after losing her only son. Her home was crowded, with many folks there to support her with condolences. But this time, there was no Earl cooking on the grill, which he learned from Benjamin. Despite her loss, Brenda proved to be a stronger woman than expected.

Shaquana and Maurice were there to hold her down, though Brenda sensed a change between them. The illumination of contentedness was nowhere upon them like she'd last seen them. Maurice was constantly stepping outside to talk on his iPhone, and Brenda caught Shaquana on more than one occasion casting looks of disapproval and suspicion.

I wonder what's going on with them two? Brenda thought as she sat on her sofa peacefully while sipping wine from a champagne flute.

"Auntie Brenda . . . do you think that they'll let Daquan attend the funeral?" Shaquana asked, sitting next to her auntie while holding her hand.

"I . . . have to . . . ," Brenda tried to speak but choked up on her tears.

"It's okay, Auntie," Shaquana said as she wrapped her arms around her.

"I'm okay. It's just too much! He was my only baby!" Brenda said, breaking down into a storm of tears.

Ms. Charmaine, an old lady who'd known Brenda since childhood, came over and wrapped her arms around her and said, "Baby, it's in God's will, and he is in God's presence. It will take time to heal. But just know that God will carry you and that he never runs out of blessings, child."

"Thank you, Ms. Charmaine."

"God has your baby, and you need not worry, hear?" she asked, hugging Brenda tightly and then planting a kiss on her forehead.

"Yes, ma'am," Brenda answered.

* * *

As the tears continued to fall, Maurice appeared back in the living room and locked eyes with Brenda for a moment. Shaquana had excused herself for a moment to use the restroom, and no one else was paying attention to their moment of soul searching. She badly didn't want to mistake the look in his eyes as sympathy, and wanted him to reach out and hold her. It was as if he'd heard her thoughts, because he was now walking toward her with his eyes locked on her.

When Maurice made it to her, he embraced her and kissed her softly on her lips. It was as if no one could see what was happening; only the two of them stood together in their erogenous zones. His lips were soft and tasted of honey as he ravished her passionately with his hallmark kiss. She let out a moan and threw her arms around his neck, intensifying the kiss on her side of the participation.

"Umm . . . ," she moaned out as her mound began to form into a sweet flood of water, causing her to climax.

"Maurice!" Brenda said as she lay her bedroom, dreaming about her niece's man.

No one was home when she came out of her dream.

Damn! she thought as she looked around and found herself alone, for the crowd had left hours ago.

"What is it with this man?" she said as she felt the sticky aftermath between her legs.

When she touched herself beneath her silk gown, her clitoris was still throbbing and needed to be attended to. Instead of pleasing herself, Brenda raised from the bed and prepared herself a hot, soothing bubble bath—at three in the morning.

* * *

Maurice and C-Murder pulled up to the residence in Savanna, Georgia, in a black Ford Taurus. The house was in a middle-class section in a quiet neighborhood.

"He's definitely here!" Maurice said from the driver's seat, seeing the state trooper car in the driveway

"Then let's go pay Carl a visit!" C-Murder said, adjusting the ski mask on his face.

Maurice followed suit, and then both of them emerged from the car and hastened to the side of the home, passing a boat and jumping over a small fence. They both were approached by two angry growling pit bulls. Before the dogs had a chance to attack, C-Murder raised his P89 silencer and popped both dogs in their heads.

Tat! Tat! Tat! Tat!

Both dogs let out a small cry and instantly fell to their deaths.

Maurice and C-Murder continued on to their business and came upon a back sliding door with an unobstructed view of the kitchen and dark home. C-Murder tucked his P89 into his back waistband and unzipped the fanny pack clamped to his waist. He reached inside and retrieved a window cutter and a suction cup.

"I love this part of the work," C-Murder said. "It's the most beautiful invention ever!"

He then placed the suction cup onto the glass near the lock and cut around the perimeter of the cup.

"I see you have good skills," Maurice said to him.

Pluck!

"Yep!" C-Murder retorted as he completed the task of removing the glass, revealing a hole big enough to slide his hand through.

C-Murder took the cut-off glass and disposed of it in the grass, and then placed his equipment back into his fanny pack.

"Let's ride, Mauri," C-Murder whispered as he proceeded to put his hand through the hole.

Out of rage, Maurice quickly jacked C-Murder up and rammed his Glock .19 to the side of C-Murder's head.

"Nigga! Don't you ever speak of names when on a mission! Do you understand me? That shit is zero tolerance, and you should know better!" Maurice said between clenched teeth.

C-Murder was unmoved and fearless, and much as he wanted to whack Maurice, he couldn't because he knew that what Maurice was telling him was true. He'd slipped up and vowed to himself to never do it again—nor to let Maurice slide if he ever placed a gun to his head again.

"I get you, man . . . and that's my fuck-up! Now, please, get that gun from my head!" C-Murder said calmly.

This nigga isn't afraid of death—death struck! Maurice thought as he pulled his weapon away.

"Let's do this!" Maurice retorted.

Together they crept through the darkness of the trashy home, with their weapons in their hands. They both took the stairs light-footedly, and once they got to the top, they heard footsteps and then the sound of a door opening.

Out walked a blonde female in her early twenties rubbing her eyes. When she saw the two figures, she let out half a scream after being popped twice in her larynx from C-Murder's P89. She dropped to her knees while holding her bloody throat, trying desperately to hold on. But C-Murder popped her twice again between her eyes, ending her life.

It is dark, and yet this nigga has 20-20 vision, Maurice thought as he stepped over the dead woman's body and walked into the room from which she had stepped out.

* * *

When Carl Galifianakis heard the short scream, he abruptly awoke from his sleep. He was no heavy sleeper like his wife, Debra, who was snoring up a storm. Carl sensed something amiss in the air and reached over to open the nightstand to retrieve his Glock .21. When he grabbed his gun, which had killed many niggas and some maniac whites, he chambered a round.

Click! Click!

Maybe Kate is getting her groove on . . . hell, not in my ho-use! Carl thought as he emerged from bed in his shit-stained
white briefs.

As soon as he made it to the entrance of his door, he heard two muffled distinctive shots hit the headboard.

"What the fuck!" Carl yelled as he squeezed his Glock blindly into the darkness of his home, refusing to take any chances, for he knew beyond a doubt that danger was upon him.

Boom! Boom! Boom!

Carl pulled the trigger repeatedly like a mad man, simultaneously backing himself into the room. His wife, Debra, who was now awake and screaming, leaped from the bed and was struck in her head twice by Maurice's Glock .19, sending her brains flying all over the wall.

"Nooo!" Carl screamed as the fire ceased.

He knew Debra was dead as soon as her screams were cut off.

"You can't win, Carl. It's over!" Maurice shouted.

"Who are you?" Carl yelled out, slouched down on the other side of his bed while reaching underneath and grabbing his M-16 rifle.

"I say . . . who are you, nigger?"

"Earl Davis . . . you forgot me already? You just killed me, Carl!" Maurice said to him as he maneuvered through the dark room, with C-Murder grabbing the wall outside in the hallway.

They both felt that the veteran had tricks up his sleeves. He was adamant and accepting death already. Maurice could bet every dollar he owned that Carl was growing homicidal and suicidal by every ticking second, and as if on cue with his predicted thoughts, Carl stood up and squeezed off a deadly fusillade of bullets, swaying his weapon from side to side.

"Motherfuckers! Come in my home, huh?" he screamed as he continued to light up the night.

Maurice dove for cover the moment he heard the first round crack.

This bitch definitely plans on going out! Maurice thought, slouched down on the other side of the bed near Debra's lifeless body.

Carl sprayed out into the hall as well, forcing C-Murder to back further out of the line of danger.

"Come on, fucker! Make my day!" Carl yelled like a mad man as he continued to squeeze.

They're waiting me out, Carl thought, with a now-empty M-16. *Fuck!*

And as if on cue, when Maurice and C-Murder heard the clicks of the empty rifle, they both swarmed the other side of the bed and shot repeatedly in Carl's direction.

Boom! Boom! Boom!

The sparks from Maurice's Glock illuminated the darkness, revealing Carl's lifeless body at every pull of the trigger.

Together, Maurice and C-Murder unloaded their weapons into Carl. They then left the gruesome scene inconspicuously. Fortunately for them, the neighbors slept through all the mayhem, making their escape smooth and complete.

Seeing how C-Murder held up in the mayhem proved to Maurice how much C-Murder was meant for action. He wanted a team of niggas like C-Murder—and he'd call the group Deathstruck!

Thanks to Google they had been able to find Carl to deliver his death sentence, and they planned to continue their spree until all involved were dead. Public records and inside connects had worked, which was no surprise to Maurice.

He didn't know Earl very well, but he was Brenda's son and only child.

Carl had had no remorse when he killed him, and now it was his entire family that had just been tossed into death for his spitefulness and dislike of blacks, Maurice thought as he accelerated his car, with C-Murder in the passenger seat, sitting there peacefully as always.

Deathstruck . . . sounds nice, Maurice thought.

* * *

The news of his cousin Earl's death had him up, unable to get any sleep. Daquan had cried nonstop, grieving for his cousin. He was looking forward to seeing Earl once he won his case. Now he was praying to be allowed to see Earl's last day on earth. He stood in the cell's doorway and stared out into the dormitory dolorously. His cellmate, Joshah, was asleep and snoring like a bear in a cave, and all Daquan could think about was him and Earl's good times. Earl was his favorite oldest cousin, who had taught him how to take a nigga to the sky in a flash of a second and slam him on his neck. It was all over the news how Earl was killed, supposedly reaching for a gun that was never found.

115

"They killed my cousin for nothing, man!" Daquan cried out, causing Joshah to wake up with an attitude and sucking his teeth.

"Hey, Daquan! Lil brah, check . . . !"

"Nigga, you mad, huh?" Daquan asked him angrily, sensing Joshah's attitude.

Joshah didn't like the tone in Daquan's voice, and although he was a CI, he was far from a pussy. He had almost let it go, being that Daquan was in a dolorous state of mind, but Daquan had challenged his ego nonchalantly.

Joshah raised up on the top bunk with only his briefs and white wifebeater on, and looked over at Daquan menacingly. "Damn, lil nigga. I understand your loss and all, but you have a cellmate that's trying to sleep . . ."

"Nigga! Fuck you and your sleep, nigga. If you got a problem, get your shit on the door!" Daquan said angrily.

"Fuck you, nigga, huh!" Joshah said fearlessly as he jumped down from the top bunk in an attempt to step in Daquan's face.

Unfortunately for Joshah, the moment his feet hit the deck, Daquan was on him like a raging lion, striking him with rapid blows. Joshah had underestimated Daquan and the rumors about how good a fighter he was, which had remained in the back of his mind until now. Daquan's first hit had him seeing stars and backed into a perilous situation. Balling up to protect himself was useless. Daquan's blows were too powerful and his uppercuts successful.

"Pussy nigga! What now, huh?" Daquan screamed out as he continued to beat down Joshah, who was very defenseless against Daquan's steady blow.

Fortunately for Joshah, the bug he had in his cell to record Daquan had picked up the scuffle and sent help immediately. The moment the cell door rolled open, Daquan had finally TKO'd Joshah, sending him to the deck face first and bloody. Before he had time to follow up, he was tackled by guards and brought down and placed in handcuffs. He was then dragged off from his cell en route to confinement.

* * *

"Damn, baby. Suck that dick!" Jarvis purred as Chinadoll sucked his dick and massaged his balls.

He called Chinadoll over to his place again since he'd been home. And he enjoyed the pleasure she gave him. She was a gorgeous Cambodian native, who stood five five, with a ridiculous ass—from taking ass injections.

He was melting in her sea of wild, exhausting sex, and she was in love with his mansion, despite the ugly bullet-wrecked scenery downstairs. She was everything that Champagne wasn't—in a good sense.

She is a real catering woman, but she is not Champagne and will never be her, Jarvis thought as he reached his load and climaxed.

"Arrgghhh, shit!" Jarvis groaned out as Chinadoll swallowed his entire load, slurping loudly on his sensitive dick.

When she was done, she made a loud pop sound effect, as if she was sucking on her favorite lollipop.

"Damn, Chinadoll! You're amazing!" Jarvis said, rubbing her long black delicate hair.

"And you are worthy, Jarvis," she retorted, with a pout on her face that turned Jarvis on. "What are your plans tonight? And I'm only asking because I want to cook for you," she said as she raised from the bed, putting on her clothes to prepare to leave soon.

Dawn would be upon her, and she had to return home to her husband, whom she'd lied to and told she'd be working late at her new job as a nurse assistant. Actually, she was off for the next two days.

"You're quiet. Does that mean you're going to be busy?" Chinadoll asked Jarvis, who was feeling bad about everything he was doing, when he was supposed to be out searching for Champagne.

But he realized that even with a compass, he'd be lost, because he had no direction of where Tameka could be.

He looked at Chinadoll, and by the scowl on her face, he could see that his muteness was bothering her.

"You turn me on when you look that beautiful!" Jarvis said.

"And you make me sick when you ignore me. Now, do you want me to come cook for you tonight?" she asked him again.

Hell! Having her cook for me won't hurt. She's enjoying herself, and so am I! Jarvis contemplated.

"Yes, beautiful. I'll be waiting. If I'm not here, help yourself in . . ."

"With what key?" she said in her native language.

"With the one I'ma give you," Jarvis responded.

He surprised her because not only did he understand her language, but he spoke it as well. A dream that he had accomplished in college.

"Damn, nigga! That is so cute!" Chinadoll exclaimed.

"And you're so beautiful," he said in Cambodian again.

"Did he just speak Cambodian? Where the fuck is that at in his file?" Clemons exclaimed, highly upset after just hearing Jarvis speak the language of his play toy.

"I seriously didn't see anything like that in his file either," Norton retorted, fumbling through Jarvis's profile.

They were sitting a block down from his mansion, in a black unmarked SUV, clearly hearing every voice and movement inside the mansion.

"Something's not adding up. I don't understand," Norton said, frustrated.

"You're damn correct! Something isn't adding up. That little mistake could mean something big and proves that the FBI knows nothing about Mr. Poole," Clemons said.

The door to the mansion opened, and Chinadoll stepped out in a hasty strut to her Audi. She hurried and started the engine, and she then flew past the unmarked SUV.

"If I could pull her over, I'd take her license," Norton said.

"Give the woman a break. She's in a hurry to get back home to her kids. You heard her. She lied to her husband," Clemons explained.

"One reason why I'm not married," Norton retorted.

"Whatever! Every woman isn't the same, Clooney!"

"Oh, I'm Clooney now?" he said.

"I guess if . . ."

Clemons stopped in mid-sentence when she heard Jarvis crying and mumbling something indiscernible. She tried to adjust the volume of the bugs but still got no clearance. It wasn't until she put two and two together that she realized that Jarvis was praying and speaking in tongues.

"He's praying," she said, with a smirk.

"That boy is going to need more than God, Clemons. And you know it!" Norton retorted.

"I don't know anything about no one's beliefs. I believe in one goddess, and that's me!" Clemons said as she smiled like the spoiled brat she was.

"Okay! Mother to God . . . come back to space, because our man is dialing out," Norton said as he listened to Jarvis dial out on his phone.

"Yo!"

"Spin . . . I need to see you, man!" Jarvis said.

"Concerning?"

"Business like always," Jarvis answered.

"I'll call you in a couple days. Same place?"

"Yeah . . . on the hill. The Spot Light closed," Jarvis informed Spin in code, to show up at his home and not the club.

"Ten-four," Spin said before he disconnected.

Sixteen

"Soon that day will come. We are going to see the King . . . Hallelujah! Hallelujah! We're going to see the King!"

As the church choir sang aloud in praise, a mile-long line paid their respects to Earl, who was lying in an all-white casket with gold trim. He was dressed in an all-white Armani tailored suit and looked like himself.

The Church of God on 12th Street in Jonesboro was full beyond its capacity and was the biggest church in town, run by Reverend Harris. Brenda was crying in the front row, but she remained strong. She was supported by Shaquana; Maurice; Katrina, who was taking it the hardest because she was pregnant with Earl's child; and Charles, who sat behind them with his wife and newborn.

It was a touching scene and more grief than one person could handle. Brenda looked up, wiped her eyes, and saw Ms. Mae pushing herself up to Earl's casket with her walker, to which she had recently become confined. At the sight of Ms. Mae, Brenda thought of Champagne.

Champagne wouldn't miss Earl's funeral, Brenda thought as she watched Ms. Mae kiss Earl on his forehead and rub his cotton-gloved hands.

Daquan was unable to attend the funeral due to his recent isolation replacement. He was considered a flight risk. When Ms. Mae walked away from the casket, Brenda's heart dropped when she saw the next person in line who had come to show her son respect. Never in a million years would she have thought to see Jerome.

Lord! Is that really him? Brenda wanted to know.

When she looked over at Shaquana and Maurice, they too seemed surprised. When Shaquana had stopped seeing Jerome coming by, Brenda had come out and told her that she and Jerome were no longer together. And not being one to press the issue, Shaquana left it at that.

When Jerome walked away from the casket, he made his way over to Brenda to support her in sympathy. As he made it to her, she broke down hysterically. Jerome grabbed her by both of her hands and brought her to her feet, embracing her tightly.

"You hurt me, Brenda. But my pain will never amount to your loss. I'm sorry and wish you the best. Just know that he's at rest now," Jerome whispered into Brenda's ear.

He then left her standing momentarily before she half-collapsed to the floor, crying hysterically. Luckily, Maurice was there to catch her fall.

"Baby! Come back! We need you!" Katrina shouted in tears.

"Lord! Why? My own baby!" Brenda shouted out as Maurice held her in his arms and sat her back down on the bench next to Shaquana, who was crying yet doing a good job at maintaining her grief.

When Maurice turned around, he saw Charles crying in his wife's arms.

"Why! Why! Why!" Brenda continued to scream as Maurice consoled her in his arms.

"It's in God's hands, Bre. He home now!" Maurice whispered in her ear, calling her by her high school nickname.

She was completely wrecked, especially after seeing how much a real man Jerome was to show up and support her.

How could I hurt him? Why Lord? He was so good to me. Now he gone! Brenda thought.

When Maurice looked beyond Charles's bench, he saw a familiar face that only he saw out of order.

What the fuck is he doing here? Maurice thought angrily as he watched Kenneth sitting in the third row with his eyes locked on Shaquana, unaware of Maurice watching him.

So now we playing them games, huh? Maurice thought, badly wanting to explode and put him and Shaquana on the spot.

But there were too many eyes, and it would ruin what he already had planned for the two lovers. Maurice was hurt, and he badly wanted to expose Shaquana and show her how stupid she was to think that he was a fool and didn't see her infidelity.

Don't worry, nigga. We all subject to death, so prepare yourself, Maurice thought as he continued to hold Brenda.

* * *

"So you telling me that you need half a billion dollars in counterfeit bills?" Spin asked Jarvis.

"Yes, man! I need it. And like I said, we could work out whatever funds . . ."

"Are you still bringing in shipments?" Spin asked Jarvis about his drug business.

Jarvis sighed before he answered a question that he was already expecting. "Since my fallout with Haitian Beny and then his incarceration, the land has been dry. Except for this nigga named Maurice who's been spreading his product . . ."

"So, there's a new nigga in town, eh?" Spin cut Jarvis off.

"Understand this, Spin . . . ," Jarvis began as he got up from his La-Z-Boy and walked over to his mini bar, where Big Shawn sat drinking a glass of Remy Martin.

"Any man who's eating in my city is because I let him," he said, pouring himself another Remy on the rocks. "There is no new man in town . . . only a guest. I chose to fall back when the feds raided Haitian Beny's mansion and save him from the death sentence that I was close to giving him . . ."

And you escaped my death sentence, motherfucker! Spin thought of the failed hit that Big Shawn orchestrated, which ended up killing rapper Antron and wounding Jarvis's girlfriend.

"So to answer your question . . . as of now, I'm on hold to protect myself and clientele," Jarvis responded.

"I understand that, Jarvis. So what are you willing to do once I accommodate you with a half billion dollars in counterfeit bills? It's not easy, son, and it's very pricey," Spin explained.

Jarvis knew that to obtain what he desperately needed, he would have to come up with top dollar. He wanted to be ready for the next time Tameka called. It had been weeks since she called, and he knew that she was doing it purposely to give him enough time.

The city wanted him to close down his establishment, but he wouldn't lose to give it up as a sacrifice.

"How about the club?" Jarvis said.

"What about the club, son?" Spin asked for verification.

"I'll sell you the club with $200,000 in cash . . ."

"Son . . . the club is a deal, but we're talking about a half billion. What is $200,000 in cash worth? That's in my pocket, son! I need a mil' to deal," Spin said.

A million dollars, really? Jarvis thought.

"How soon you get the funds to me and the necessary documents?" Spin asked.

Jarvis took a sip of his drink and then looked at his Rolex to check the time.

"I could send you back with the million, but I'll need to get with my attorney on Monday to have the necessary documents ready."

"That sits well with me, son," Spin said, standing up and then walking toward the front door to depart. "Call me when you're ready to hand over our deal, and I'll be here to pick it up."

"Let's go, Shawn," Spin continued as they walked out the door, unaware of the FBI agents watching.

* * *

Cuban Black and Tameka were having a delicious dinner at a seafood restaurant in Palm Beach, which was her hometown that she deserted to live a better life and escape from her abusive boyfriend. She never intentionally expected her life to transform the way it had, from poverty to lavishness, from driving bad conditioned Hondas to being chauffeured around like a queen in luxurious limos. She had to give all thanks and gratitude to a dead man for making it all possible—Benjamin.

Sitting across from her in his all-black Versace suit and excessive use of Valentino Uomo cologne, she admired Cuban Black. She loved the way he sucked the butter from the snow crabs after dipping them in his bowl of melted butter. He reminded her so much of Benjamin.

Maybe he is Benjamin, Tameka thought preposterously, shoving a friend shrimp into her mouth.

"Thank you for bringing me here, Cuban Black," she said gently and seductively.

"It's a pleasure for your gratification. I owe it to you," he retorted, wiping his mouth.

Tameka saw that he had missed a spot in the right corner, and grabbed a napkin.

She reached across the table, wiped away the food, and said, "You missed a spot!"

When Cuban Black grabbed her hand, she flinched from being startled, thinking that he didn't like for a woman to touch him. But she was wrong. Instead of a rejection, Cuban Black turned her hand palm down and kissed the top of her hand like she was a noble queen. She was obsessed with his sweet affection and couldn't help but blush.

"Thank you, baby gal. You're so kind and sweet. I think I'm 'bout to go back on my own principle," he exclaimed.

"And what is that, Cuban Black?" Tameka asked him with feigned perplexity on her face as he began to caress her delicate hair.

"I told myself for years that to mix pleasure with business would never work . . . like oil and water . . ."

"And didn't I tell you that your principle didn't exist in my world . . . and that what I want, I get?" she said, snatching her hand back and clamping her hands on her hips with a sexy pout on her face.

Damn, she's beautiful! Cuban Black thought as his manhood betrayed him. Unbeknownst to Tameka, Cuban Black purposely left the food in the corner of his mouth to see if she was woman enough to clean up after him. She passed the test, just like every other test he tossed her way.

"Don't look like that . . ."

Then, nigga, stop playing with me . . . and fuck the shit out of me! Tameka wanted to say to him.

"Then stop making me look like this!"

"How am I supposed to stop it?" Cuban Black said, with a smile on his face, egging her on.

"How 'bout we talk 'bout our business first. Then we'll figure out how to play later," Tameka suggested.

"Damn! I love your attitude, baby gal!" he retorted.

He brought her to Palm Beach to avoid being seen with her in Miami, for he wanted her to remain low key from those who were watching and trying to figure out him and his millionaire organization. Cuban Black was always five moves ahead of his adversaries. That's why he was using his queen to destroy them one by one.

Before anyone can figure it out, it will be too late . . . because the death queen will be done with her death list soon. My beautiful villainess, he thought.

"Miami Gardens. He goes by the name Lorel Saint Paul. People call him Saint. He is a standout, flashy, flamboyant individual whose downfall is pussy. I want him and his crew wiped out. He is a future threat to our organization and one of Beny's men!" Cuban Black explained.

"It's said . . . then it's done, Cuban Black," Tameka seductively answered, taking a sip of her Kim Crawford wine while looking into his eyes.

* * *

Dear Lord! Please come rescue me from this perilous situation. Forgive me for all of my sins, Lord . . . , Champagne paused for a moment to gather her thoughts in prayer.

She was on her knees leaning across her bed with her eyes closed, unaware of the lights being cut off and the rapist creeping up on her. He had his own key to her door and the skills to move swiftly like the artisan professional assassin he was.

"Please, Father. God . . . protect me, and free me from my captives. Let me repent from my wrongdoing, and live."

At the distinctive sound of knees being popped, Champagne's eyes flung open, and darkness was revealed to her.

No! she thought timorously.

Champagne quickly slid across the bed while simultaneously feeling underneath her pillow for her homemade weapon that she had fashioned from a nail she found in the bathroom under the sink.

Come on, bitch! she thought as she grabbed hold of the extremely sharp nail. She felt him feel for her on the bed, but couldn't see him.

Damn it! he thought as he swung blindly in hopes of catching his prey, but he came up short, unbeknownst to him, by an inch.

Run to the bathroom now! Champagne's conscience screamed out to her.

It was her only hope besides the nail to escape her attacker, and she went for it. Her attacker must have heard her contemplated thoughts, because he was on her heels as she made a dash for the bathroom. En route, she tripped on her long gown, stumbled, and fell to the ground, causing her attacker to stumble over her.

"Shit!" he exclaimed in an irrefutable Haitian accent.

No! Champagne thought as his hands grabbed a fistful of her hair.

"Please no!" she yelled out, swinging her hands wildly with the nail, trying to find the rapist's face. But he was too strong and began to drag her to the bed by her hair.

"Be good, bitch! Don't make me mad!" he said to her as he wrapped his hand around her throat.

"Nooooo!" Champagne managed to squeeze out as the rapist throttled her.

Her chance had favorably presented itself, for she moved with desperate agility and dug the nail into his face and sliced him twice and deep.

"Bitch!" he screamed out loud in pain as he instantly let go of her.

She took her last chance wisely and made a dash for the bathroom again—this time succeeding. Once inside, she closed the door and locked it as she then began to pray out loud.

"Please, Lord, save me. Turn him away from me and never let him return," Champagne prayed for twenty minutes before she realized that the rapist was no longer with her. She closed her eyes, not wanting to chance the darkness so soon, and fell asleep fitfully on the bathroom floor.

* * *

"Yes, daddy! Beat this pussy up!" Tameka screamed out in ecstasy as Cuban Black penetrated her womb with rapid strokes.

Her legs were locked behind his back as he drove deeper inside her, and her nails dug into his back. She was calling him daddy, allowing him to have his way with her.

"This what you want, huh?" Cuban Black asked her.

"Yes! Yes! Yes! Daddy . . . fuck the shit out of me!" she screamed as he sped up his pace, slamming his enormous love tool inside her excessively wet pussy.

Her eyes were rolling to the back of her head, and she was loving every thrust.

Damn! This dick is one of a kind! she thought as she continued to moan out loud.

She quickly realized that all the men she had weren't fucking her like she intended. She thought that she was being fucked, but they were making love to her—something that she was running from. K-Zoe had come close to fucking her like Cuban Black was, but his last few times, he was trying to be sweet with the love making.

And a bitch just doesn't have time for that. I need to be fucked good, with no damn attachments. The same thing as Cuban Black wants! Tameka thought as she came to an electrifying orgasm.

"Ummm, shit!" she purred out loud as Cuban Black erupted his load as well.

As he came, he pulled out and shot his load all over Tameka's belly and pretty caramel breasts.

"Uhh!" he exhaled, stroking his load onto her as she began to play in it like a naughty girl.

"Damn! That dick good, daddy!" she said, exhausted.

"And that pussy is too much, baby gal!" Cuban Black said breathlessly as he collapsed on the hotel bed next to her.

Both of them were so overworked. Tameka cleaned herself off and then snuggled next to him in bed.

Seventeen

Coco sat in a soothing bubble bath relaxing and waiting on K-Zoe to come in. Despite catching him and her grimy-ass boss, Tameka, fucking, she concealed her hurt and slowly planned on making both of them pay.

Two bitches can play dirty, home girl! Coco thought as she took a sip from her wine glass.

She was stress-free and ready to make K-Zoe pay with his life.

"After tonight, K-Zoe won't know what pussy ever felt like!" Coco said to herself as she then began laughing as if she was overtaken by demons.

Tameka had created a monster, unbeknownst to her, and like a pit bull, she would suddenly turn on her owner.

Coco was ready to terminate her creator—Tameka.

* * *

"Yo, Saint! It's K-Zoe and his people!" one of Haitian Saint's lieutenants named Johnny screamed out.

Inside the relatively small mansion in Miami Gardens was the usual crew who had the place tagged and regulated under Haitian Beny's connection with the Zo'pound gang.

Saint was a muscular and flashy, dark-skinned, five foot eight Haitian who used to be an assassin for the gang, until Haitian Beny recruited him to his force. It was Haitian Beny who made it heaven for a lot of niggas like Saint.

And despite his love, Saint wasn't keeping it real with Beny, which was why Cuban Black had ordered him dead—the same as Tankhead. It wasn't because of their lack of loyalty to Haitian Beny that he wanted them dead; it went deeper than anyone would think. Cuban Black was always prepared for the domino fall effect. He had known Haitian Beny for a long time, but he still didn't know what any man would do in his position, so he played it safe. Every man in Haitian Beny's organization had to go.

As K-Zoe and Coco strutted through the door, they quickly took a head count and saw that there were six men altogether and three strippers performing for the extra cash.

"What's up, K-Zoe and Mrs. K-Zoe?" Saint said as he greeted them with a handshake and gentle kiss on her delicate hand, respectively.

Saint spoke in a deep accent and had great English from growing up in Miami his whole life, after leaving Haiti at the age of three. All he knew growing up in Little Haiti were drugs and slaughter.

"We're chilling! Just coming to see what's up with that three-piece so we can flex," K-Zoe said.

Saint looked at Coco, who was carrying a black duffel bag and was dressed in an all-black Gucci sweat suit. Despite her tomboyish appearance, her delicate curves were still accentuating the Gucci set.

"That's right! Let's handle business," Saint retorted as he looked over toward the den where a stripper and her friend lay on top of a pool table eating each other out while his crew of five men looked on, throwing cash at the table.

"Yo, Rosco!" Saint yelled toward the den, getting the attention of one of his sergeants.

"What's good, Saint?" Rosco responded.

He was a tall, lanky man with an addiction to Molly and tricking. Despite his addition, he was a go-getter for Saint and a hit man as well. He wasn't Haitian, but he was like family to all of them.

"I need you to come to the back with me," Saint said as Rosco approached him with a hefty wad in his hands.

"That's cool!" Rosco answered as he followed Saint with K-Zoe and Coco to the back.

He couldn't help but stare at Coco's succulent ass bouncing in her sweat pants. He was trying his best to respect K-Zoe and not lust after his woman, but the bitch was supermodel bad.

The four of them walked down a hallway, swung a left into another hallway, and shortly stopped in front of an iron doorway.

Saint quickly accessed a code that allowed them entrance by rapidly punching in an eight-digit number. Everyone then stepped into a room full of firepower. Attached to racks on all walls hung AK-47s, M-16s, Mini-14s, and Mac-10s, among every other type of handgun a person could possibly think of.

"It's all here, K-Zoe. Whatever you need. All clean of bodies!" Saint said, advertising his business as he spun around, preening.

The room was also sound-proof and had a small gun range in it. K-Zoe and Coco separated and walked toward the collection of guns and picked up two Glock .17s.

"These bad boys come with any silencers?" K-Zoe asked as he slid back to check the weapon for ammo.

"We have them, but only a couple left and . . . ," Saint began with emphasis, dragging out his last words, "they are hard to come across and pricey at the moment . . ."

"How many do you have? Money isn't an issue, Saint," K-Zoe said as he turned around and caught Rosco mesmerized while looking at Coco's ass.

"Rosco . . . grab me them three silencers . . ."

"And some bullets for these, because I want to test drive them," Coco added, causing Rosco and Saint to look at her in surprise, which was written all over their faces.

"What! A bitch can't pull a trigger? I don't see any rules or regulations!" she said sassily and sexily, looking around for any woman prohibition signs.

When both men looked at K-Zoe, they saw him with a smirk on his face.

"What? The woman wants to feel what she came for," K-Zoe said with a grin.

"And that's no problem. Rosco . . . grab the silencers and a box of hollows," Saint demanded.

Rosco followed orders and retrieved three silencers and a box of hollow-point bullets from a back room. He then stepped back after he laid the items on the wooden table that sat in the middle of the room.

"Nice!" K-Zoe said as he placed a set of gloves on his hands that he pulled from the duffel bag. Coco followed suit and then began to load the two Glock .17s.

"Let me remind you that these aren't semis. They are fully automatics. Everything you see in here," Saint explained to the duo as he sparked up a Newport cigarette.

I hate those stank-ass cigarettes, Coco thought as she loaded her weapons and then slammed both clips into the Glocks.

K-Zoe was screwing on one of the silencers, when he heard two shots erupt behind him.

Boom! Boom!

"What the fuck!" Saint screamed, dropping his cigarette from his trembling lips as he stared at Rosco's still-standing, bloody, bullet-wrecked face.

Boom! Boom! Boom!

Coco fired three more times, hitting Rosco in his chest and finally getting the dead man to fall.

"Hey, man, what she doing?" Saint frantically screamed.

"She's testing out the weapons. What does it look like?" K-Zoe said as he pointed his Glock at Saint and squeezed off the entire clip into his chest.

Coco stood over Saint's body and hit him twice more in the face.

Boom! Boom!

"Damn, nigga! How we goin' to get out of here?" Coco asked in panic, still holding her smoking gun.

"If I didn't know how, do you think he'd be dead?"

"Load as many handguns as you can," he retorted, tossing over the empty duffel bag to Coco as he hit the safe in the back office.

After punching in the same eight-digit access code to the safe, K-Zoe grabbed a bagful of money from inside.

"Jackpot!" he exclaimed.

In a matter of minutes, the both of them loaded all the handguns they could into the duffel bag and then proceeded to make their escape.

Being that the bag had a little too much weight for Coco to be carrying, K-Zoe decided to take it and give her the two silencers.

"Make sure you pop everything in sight, baby. No hesitation!" he said as he punched in the code that he had memorized simply by watching Saint.

"How the fuck did you catch it? That nigga punched it in like eighty miles per hour," Coco inquired, impressed.

"One thing I've always been good at, baby, is numbers."

"And breaking a bitch's heart!" Coco said angrily.

"What do you mean by that?" K-Zoe said as they walked through the door and down the hall.

"Never mind me. Just know that I don't miss shit, K-Zoe!" she retorted as they turned the corner.

The sound of ass cheeks being slapped could be heard over the 2 Chains music.

With both silencers in her hands as she came in sight of the crew in the den, Coco and K-Zoe quickly realized that more company had joined the party. There were now six in the den, standing around the pool table watching the intense foreplay the strippers were giving each other.

Shit, I only expected four! she thought as she aimed and squeezed.

Tat! Tat! Tat! Tat!

The muffled shots helped her seize the advantage and allowed her to knock off three quickly.

"Oh shit!" one guard screamed as blood splattered on his face from the impact of the hollow points penetrating his partner's skull.

The strippers screamed hysterically in the background as Coco popped another one of the guards, who was reaching underneath his shirt for his weapon, twice.

K-Zoe had the last two in his line, but missed the second one, who ducked behind the pool table and then returned fire.

Boom! Boom! Boom!

The two .44 Bulldogs resounded and almost scared Coco to death as she scrambled for cover with K-Zoe.

Fuck! she thought.

Hearing the screams of the stripers was making her instincts respond slowly. As well, the man with the .44 Bulldogs must have felt the same way, because he turned the gun on both strippers.

Boom! Boom! Boom! Boom!

There were no more screams, just the three gun slangers fighting for the win.

"Damn, K-Zoe. What's up, man?" the man yelled out in Creole.

All Coco could make out was K-Zoe's name.

K-Zoe knew the Haitian man as Bo, who he grew up with in Little Haiti, but today, Bo was a little perplexed. The last time he checked, he and K-Zoe were on the same team. But not today! K-Zoe had a mission to complete.

"Bo . . . you a good man. Come out! I don't want you, man. We go way back. Stay out of this!" K-Zoe demanded, attempting to wile Bo from behind the pool table.

From time to time, K-Zoe peeped around the concrete wall that was protecting him and Coco as they looked for an escape route.

"Man, why you acting up, man?" Bo screamed.

"Bo . . . stay out of this shit, man. Walk free . . ."

Boom! Boom! Boom!

"Fuck you, nigga! You intended to kill me, too!" Bo screamed out hysterically in Creole after shooting toward the wall.

Coco couldn't understand shit, and she was growing impatient as the dialogue between them intensified.

"Bo . . . I'ma toss my weapons out and let you see we good, man!" K-Zoe said as he dug into the duffel bag.

What the hell is he doing? Coco thought.

K-Zoe grabbed four Glock .19s and tossed them onto the floor, where they glided a half distance from Bo.

Bait! Coco thought, catching on to K-Zoe's intentions.

K-Zoe and Coco heard the sound of Bo's feet moving, and as if on cue, they both came from behind the wall firing away.

Bo was hit before he could squeeze off any shots. Together, K-Zoe and Coco ran down on Bo and filled the big man's body with hollows.

As K-Zoe continued to pull while biting on his bottom lip, Coco turned her gun on him and aimed at his head. When he looked up at her, she squeezed repeatedly and ruthlessly until both Glocks clicked empty.

"You niggas don't know when you got something good, until it's gone, grimy-ass nigga!" she said as she stepped over K-Zoe's lifeless body.

She quickly gathered the guns and the duffel bag, and then she made her escape with the sack of money.

* * *

D-Zoe was rubbing the sixteen stitches on the ugly scar on his face, when he saw only Coco making her way out of Saint's mansion.

Where the fuck is K-Zoe? he thought as he gunned the SUV's engine and halted in front of Coco, who immediately hopped inside.

"Where's K-Zoe?" D-Zoe asked.

"D-Zoe . . . they killed K-Zoe! It went wrong. They ambushed him, but I got every last one of them. I promise! They killed my baby!" Coco cried out with her hands in her face and head down in her lap.

"Shit!" D-Zoe yelled, hitting the steering wheel hard before pulling off like a maniac.

He heard the rapid gunfire, but he only thought that it was Coco and K-Zoe putting in work. The last thing he ever would have thought was that K-Zoe was in trouble.

"Damn it! How the fuck did he slip?" D-Zoe screamed as tears for his homie fell from his eyes. Unable to stand the grief, D-Zoe pulled over at a McDonald's and wept like never before.

"D-Zoe . . . they killed my baby!" Coco said as she reached out and hugged him.

Together they cried in each other's arms.

"It's okay, Coco. It's more of them niggas about to lay down with my nigga," D-Zoe promised.

RIP, dog-ass nigga! Coco thought, with a smile on her face that she hid from D-Zoe.

Eighteen

The news of K-Zoe's death had Tameka on edge. She was in her bed, pillow talking with Cuban Black when D-Zoe and Coco showed up at her luxurious beach house. D-Zoe no longer stayed nights with her due to her attempts to pull away from their sexual fling.

Looking at him sitting at her mini bar with a sad expression on his face, she saw the love he had for K-Zoe. It was on another level than what she'd seen before.

Damn! He's hurt! she thought, observing D-Zoe with the sixteen stitches that resulted from a club brawl between him and an adversary, who sliced him with a razor blade.

When she looked over at Coco, who was sitting on her plush sofa and sipping on straight Remy with no chaser, Tameka saw that she was also grieving. Tameka felt that it was her job as a boss to remind them of their subjectability to death.

"Listen, Coco and D-Zoe . . . we lost a team player . . ."

Yeah, I bet, bitch! There's no team in your eyes when you go around fucking people's men! Coco thought, almost speaking her mind aloud to Tameka. *But there is a time for everything*, she realized.

"We can't let this make us feeble. We all are subject to death and must not dwell on it. Coco . . . I want you to make sure K-Zoe go out in style . . ."

How about you do it? Wasn't you fucking him, too? Coco badly wanted to shout out, but instead shook her head and responded, "You know I am going to make sure my baby good."

"D-Zoe . . . I want you to lay low for a couple weeks. Too many people know your bond with K-Zoe and will begin to get skeptical."

"And where will I lay low?" he asked.

Didn't you kick me out to slow down our romance, and now you're talking about laying low! D-Zoe contemplated.

D-Zoe kept quiet, as he didn't want to put his business out in front of Coco, who, unbeknownst to him, already knew about Tameka's sudden disinterest in him.

"You are welcome to stay here . . . in the guest room," Tameka offered with emphasis.

"Guest room, huh?" D-Zoe said nonchalantly while sucking his teeth.

No! He did not just do that! Tameka thought angrily.

"Being that we're all a little air-tight, D-Zoe, I'ma make sure I forget that you just disrespected me . . ."

"Listen, Meka! Call it what you want, but D-Zoe don't mind nothing you want to talk. Let's go back in the room, and don't be trying to stunt on me in front of nobody!" D-Zoe said in a raging fit, beating his chest like a gorilla.

"Ummm . . . I'll see you tomorrow, Meka. I need some alone time," Coco said as she stood up to leave, but mostly to allow Meka and D-Zoe to settle their problems between themselves.

"Okay, Coco. I will call you in a few hours. Be safe and low key," Tameka said, with her back to her while staring daggers at D-Zoe, who stood his ground.

"I will, Meka," Coco said sadly before departing.

When the door had closed, the two resumed their verbal beef.

"You have some fucking nerve, D-Zoe. Who the fuck do you think you're talking to?" Tameka screamed as she clamped her hands on her hips and slanted her eyes devilishly, which was a turn-on for D-Zoe.

Damn! I love it when she looks like that, he thought as he surveyed her delicate curves, accentuated through her pink silk Prada robe.

Instead of answering, D-Zoe held a smirk on his face and then sucked his teeth again.

"Nigga! You still trying me, huh?" Tameka yelled out in range while charging D-Zoe, who leaped from his seat at the mini bar and grabbed her by her face.

Vigorously, D-Zoe kissed her, sliding his yearning tongue inside her mouth.

"Umm!" she moaned out with little resistance, for she always loved the way D-Zoe kissed her.

He backed her up to her sofa and stripped away her robe, beneath which she wore sexy lingerie that D-Zoe tore away like a deranged man.

"D-Zoe!" she called out panting, realizing that she wanted him more than she thought she did.

I can't! she thought, wanting to put an end to their romance. *But I can't! He's too sweet and obsessed.*

When she felt D-Zoe's tongue on her clitoris, swirling in a figure eight, she gave in completely and wrapped her legs around his neck while arching her back.

"Damn it, D-Zoe! I hate you! Damn! I fucking hate you!" she purred out in ecstasy. "That's right, nigga! Eat this pussy like you know I hate you!"

* * *

The club was out of his hands now, and he was now waiting for the other part of his deal, which was receiving the other half of his half billion dollars in counterfeit bills.

Jarvis was upset because Spin hadn't informed him before the deal was sealed that he wouldn't receive the half billion all at once. It had been three days since he last spoke with Spin, and two long weeks since he talked with Tameka, who he expected to be calling any day now. His frustration mostly came from Spin's sudden monkey wrench thrown into his plans of being prepared.

Jarvis then heard knocking at his door as he took a sip from his Remy bottle and quickly dismissed his thoughts of Spin's bad business.

Who the hell is this at this time of night? Jarvis wondered as he looked at his Rolex and struggled with the time due to his blurry vision.

At that moment, he realized how inebriated he was. Lately, it was all he did, when not taking out his sexual frustrations on Chinadoll—who didn't mind it one bit. He was simply giving her what her husband could not.

As he staggered to the door, he knew that it couldn't be Chinadoll.

Knock! Knock! Knock!

"Hold on! God damn it! I'm coming!" Jarvis said sluggishly as he disengaged the locks and then swung open the door.

When he saw who it was, Jarvis rubbed his eyes to make sure he wasn't tripping. Her beauty was extremely scintillating, but he knew that she was no good for him. She was dressed in a sexy mini dress and heels that propped her sexy thighs out.

This bitch is deadly gorgeous! Jarvis thought as he stared at Agent Clemons.

"You again? What do you want?" Jarvis spoke in a sluggish voice.

Agent Clemons could smell the Remy strong on his breath as she fanned the horrible smell with her hands.

"Somebody's wasted!" she said.

"Woman! I mean captain. What do you want?"

Before Jarvis could finish, Clemons forced herself into his home and walked to his bar with clanking heels. Jarvis just stood there at the doorway dumbfounded.

I know this bitch ain't just invade my trap! Jarvis reflected as he closed the door and turned around to see Clemons helping herself to a drink.

"You okay? I mean . . ." Jarvis was cut short of his senses when Clemons hopped up on the bar stool and revealed almost all her goodies.

Damn! Baby fine! he thought as she pulled down her mini dress to cover herself.

"Jarvis . . . listen to me and hear me good," Clemons began as she sincerely looked Jarvis in the eyes. "It's only me and you . . . and I'm off the clock. I'ma be real with you. I don't want to be the one bringing your door down again. Them people want your life, Jarvis, and you are . . ."

The sound of Jarvis's ringing iPhone stopped Clemons from talking. He pulled his phone out and looked at the unlisted number.

Tameka! He thought anxiously.

145

"Excuse me," Jarvis said as he answered the phone and hastened upstairs to take the call he had been waiting for.

He answered the moment he made it to his room, after stumbling twice with his balance.

"Hello!"

"Someone sounds ready," Tameka's voice came over the phone.

"I . . . I . . . I . . . I'm . . . ," Jarvis stuttered.

"Are you pulling my leg?" Tameka said as she paced in her living room.

D-Zoe was asleep in her bedroom and snoring like a bear.

When Jarvis had said he was ready, she froze in her tracks.

"No, Tameka! I'm ready. I have the half billion. All I need is a location and my baby, Tameka. Please tell me that Champagne is okay?" He said sluggishly and loud enough for anyone within earshot to hear, when he realized that his front door was wide open.

"Jarvis! Tomorrow I will let you speak to her, now that you've told me you have my money. If you're playing games, just know that I will drink all of my Champagne," Tameka teased, meaning every word of her threat.

Damn! Spin! Jarvis thought.

"Meka . . . it's there! Everything!" Jarvis retorted to a dead line.

"Hello?" he called, getting no direct reply and dead silence.

"Damn it, bitch! I hate it when you do that shit!" Jarvis exclaimed.

When he walked back downstairs, Jarvis saw that Clemons was gone.

"Great! Bitch couldn't wait for five minutes. Lord knows I was gonna get that pussy by all means tonight!" he said as he collapsed on the plush sofa.

"I'm coming to get you, baby!" Jarvis said as he then closed his eyes so that he would be sober when talking to Champagne.

* * *

The FBI was going crazy after just hearing Tameka and Jarvis's conversation. Agent Clemons was immediately told to abort her mission to try to seduce Jarvis to give up the information they now had. Team A was directed by Clemons and was assembled from their beds to get briefed on the emergency matter at hand.

"We have a person, but we now need a direction. Champagne Robinson is being held as a hostage by this Tameka Rowland," Clemons said to the conference room full of more than a dozen agents assigned to Team A.

"We have no direction, people. She could be anywhere. The last couple days, we've gathered information in the field on Tameka Rowland. She's the ex-lover of Mr. Poole, as well as ex-lover to a man who was found dead in her apartment that she abandoned and to which she never returned. He was gunned down by her at-the-time boyfriend, the now-deceased Benjamin Clark, who was believed to have been killed by Jarvis."

"When do we bring him down?" an agent asked while looking at the side-by-side mugshots of Tameka and Jarvis on a massive screen in front of the room.

"He's bait to find Tameka . . . who will lead us to Champagne. Tomorrow, we will wait on Tameka to give Jarvis instructions to bring the half billion dollars to her," Clemons said as she nodded her head to Norton to speak.

"People . . . we are close to bringing Champagne Robinson home. And then we will take Mr. Poole and his associates down as well. We must move with caution because with every move we make after this meeting, a young woman's life is in our hands to protect," Norton explained.

"People . . . this new operation is called Two Wrongs, None Right . . . and we are serving to bring these two wrongs down!" Clemons yelled with so much enthusiasm that the room exploded in exhilaration and an ovation of clapping and whistle-blowing.

"Let's get these motherfuckers and teach them who to play with . . . and not the FBI!" Clemons screamed over the ovation as she stormed out of the room with her partner.

In the hallway on the way to their offices, Agent Norton was reading a text coming in from Director Bernie Scott that put a smile on his face—that Clemons didn't miss.

"What got you smiling at five o'clock in the morning? Only a booty call could bring that result."

At the mention of "booty call," she realized how long it had been since she had a man make love to her.

Damn! It's been awhile! she thought.

"Really? To be honest, my wife is okay for at least a week . . ."

"Oh yeah. You Superman her, Norton? You'll fool the best!" Clemons said.

"Nah, Batman," Norton answered, getting a laugh out of Clemons.

"Scott just texted me this," Norton said, showing Clemons the text that read:

Scott: 8:30 a.m. You and Clemons report to Atlanta Federal Holding. Mr. Beny St. Clair is requesting to offer some valuable information. You two are doing a wonderful job. Keep it up.

"Well, I'll be damned!" Clemons said, more elated.

"They say hard work always pays off. I'm betting you a bottle of champagne that he's ready to tell us everything, even about him and Cuban Black," Norton suggested.

"I'd be stupid to bet you, Norton, so I'll pass. But I can still go for a drink. Dawn won't be here for two hours, and I want to be relaxed when we hear what Beny has to offer us," Clemons said.

"Let's go!" Norton exclaimed.

* * *

Kenneth stayed in bed just tossing and turning all night, with Shaquana on his mind. Every time he was with her, they were growing more intimate.

She is constantly in denial, but I know she wants me, Kenneth thought as he felt his throbbing erection badly wanting to burst through his briefs.

He and his baby mama, Trish, were no longer together, although he missed her gorgeous beauty. She was just too much and couldn't meet his expectations. She was a hoodlum that he regretted fucking without protection. But he loved his daughter, Miracle, unconditionally. His feelings for Trish were still in his heart, but his interest in Shaquana had gotten in the way of him considering working out their differences.

Kenneth was unable to resist the urge as he pulled out his erect penis and closed his eyes while stroking himself. He imagined making slow love to Shaquana in missionary style while she called out his name and clawed his back.

"Damn, Shaquana, girl! I love you," Kenneth purred as he sped up the pace of his strokes while masturbating.

He couldn't wait for dawn to come so he could see his secret admirer.

"Arrgghhh! Shit!" Kenneth groaned out as he exploded and climaxed heavily on his sheets and himself. "Damn! I got to get Maurice out of the way!" he said breathlessly and determinedly.

Nineteen

The loud music erupted from the alarm clock on the nightstand at 7:00 a.m. Shaquana was extremely tired, so she reached over and slammed her hand down on the snooze button. She looked over at Maurice, who was sound asleep. She badly wanted to snuggle up against him, but she was upset with his behavior lately. He had come home late again the night before and didn't bother to wake her.

He's seeing someone else. I just know it! she thought as she emerged from bed and prepared herself for school.

Two more weeks . . . and this shit will be over with. Then off to Ms. Officer I go! she thought as she stepped into the bathroom and stripped out of her sexy boy shorts. She then stepped into the hot steaming shower.

School doesn't start until 9:00 a.m., so I'll fix Maurice some breakfast and then leave to meet Ken, she thought as she adjusted the temperature of the water.

"Now that feels good!"

As she showered, Shaquana thought about Kenneth. They were spending too much time together as friends, and she was tired of feeling like she was cheating on Maurice. Deep down, she felt that Maurice knew about him.

Too many close-to-home hints, she thought. *I need to tell him, and really soon.*

When Shaquana completed her routine morning shower, she dried herself off and then walked into her bedroom with a towel wrapped around her body and one on her head.

Maurice was no longer in his deep sleep or in bed. It perplexed Shaquana because it was something new that he'd recently started doing.

"Maurice!" Shaquana screamed out, already knowing that her man was nowhere in the suite.

I hate when he does that, she reflected as she slid into sexy lingerie, black heels, and a purple backless blouse.

As she was putting in her gold hoop earrings, her iPhone alerted her that she had a text coming in. Shaquana anxiously walked over to her nightstand, grabbed her phone, and read the text with a smile on her face.

Mauri: Good morning, sunshine. I hope that you have a good day today. I feel that it's a special day. Celebration on me. I love you, baby. Trust me, there's no one in the world who'll love you like Mauri. I plan to prove that by all means. Mines forever XO

Shaquana was touched by the text from her man, so she texted him back immediately.

Quana: We will have a special day if you say so. I love you too, and don't forget to stop by Auntie Brenda's to see if she needs anything.

Mauri: I will do that after I go see Daquan. He's in court today.

Damn! How the hell did that slip by me? Today is his suppression hearing, and my ass thought to look good for the next nigga, Shaquana thought as she laid down her phone on the nightstand and resumed embellishing herself.

As she clamped on her Rolex and other conspicuous jewelry, another text alert sounded off, indicating that she had an incoming text.

"Damn it!" she exclaimed, after applying her lip liner to accentuate her cherry-red lipstick.

Shaquana hastened over to the nightstand and retrieved her iPhone and then checked her incoming text, with another smile on her face after seeing who it was.

Teacher: Good morning. I'm just hopping out the shower. I'll be waiting on you, gorgeous.

"That boy is a mess!" Shaquana said as she walked back over to her mirror at the dresser to resume her beauty regimen.

I can't wait until we're on the force together. Maybe we'll be partners as well, Shaquana thought of her and Kenneth's future as law enforcement officers while working on her eyelashes.

* * *

As FBI agents Clemons and Norton walked through the doors to the visitation room, they saw their expected visitor bound to a wheelchair and restrained only by handcuffs.

"Looks like my friend has gained a couple pounds," Norton said to Haitian Beny.

"Looks can be deceiving, agent, so please take heed and don't forget," Beny retorted.

"How are you, Beny?" Clemons asked.

Her start as the good cop began, but Haitian Beny was aware of it and simply smiled. Beny was accustomed to the interrogation techniques and quickly set the record straight.

"Listen, I called you guys, so there's no need to play good cop, bad cop roles . . . because it's useless," he explained.

"Okay, so what is it you have to tell me and my partner that has us out here?" Norton asked while placing a tape recorder on the round table.

"What's the meaning of that?" Haitian Beny asked, confused.

"This is a federal case . . . and you know how the feds operate. We already have a 100 percent case against any suspect that's picked up . . . and thanks to devices like this," Norton said while patting the recorder softly. "We break cases with no problem. Now let's talk, Beny."

Haitian Beny looked from Clemons to Norton and then released a long sigh before he spoke. "For years now, the Miami authorities have been trying to indict a man named Victor Martinez."

Holy crap! Norton thought ecstatically at the mention of Martinez's name.

Clemons looked over at Norton, who had victory written all over his face. She stomped on his foot, which was an indication for him to play it cool and let the suspect spill the beans on his own will.

Norton quickly gathered himself together, and instead of drilling Haitian Beny, he let Beny spill the beans.

"Does this Victor Martinez go by any street name, Beny?" Clemons asked, getting a moment of silence out of Beny before he spoke.

"Yeah! They call him Cuban Black! And he's my partner."

* * *

Two hours later, Haitian Beny was back in his isolation cell. He hated giving up Cuban Black and the grimy bitch

Tameka, but it had to be done. The silent tears that fell from his eyes couldn't explain the burdensome pain of betrayal. Once he received the news from his outside connect to the Zo'pound gang that all his main men were being slain, he knew that Cuban Black had given up on him and replaced him with Tameka. He had given the FBI everything they needed to bring down Cuban Black, in exchange for his freedom.

They need me to testify, and I need my freedom, Beny thought as he wiped tears from his face.

Once I'm released, I will kill Tameka myself and then Cuban Black and his family, Haitian Beny thought. He knew that what he had done was wrong and went against all the rules of the street. But he couldn't care less because he wasn't planning on returning to the streets. He was planning to die by principle, something that was expected of a snitch.

The last thing Haitian Beny wanted to do was spend the rest of his life in prison, so he made up a master escape plan to gain his freedom. To him, most victories were won by making a sacrifice, and Cuban Black was his best sacrifice. He was aware of Big Funk's and Corey's betrayal, going against him in exchange for ten years. It hurt him badly, but they too had used him as a sacrifice, and they would never expect Beny to see daylight again.

But they are wrong, Beny thought as he stood out of his chair and sat on his bed.

Many people thought he was confined to a wheelchair, but they were wrong. It had been months since he had healed and was able to walk on his own again.

The only guy who was man enough to stand strong against the system was Romel, and I will do whatever it takes

155

to make sure he walks the streets again! Haitian Beny thought as he lay back on his bunk and closed his eyes.

"It's almost over, shawty . . . almost," he said.

* * *

After eating breakfast, Kenneth had convinced Shaquana to skip a day of class and chill with him. At first, she was adamant, but then she thought about how far she was in school. She had never missed a day, so one sick day wouldn't hurt. They were at the Lenox Mall in Atlanta, sitting at a dining table at a KFC. The pancakes at IHOP nearby didn't fulfill their hunger, so they opted for a chicken sandwich with mashed potatoes and gravy.

"Damn! This sandwich is so delicious!" Shaquana exclaimed, with a mouth full of chicken.

"Really!" he responded.

"What?"

"Where's your ghetto manners if not none?" Kenneth asked her in a jesting manner.

"Sorry," she said, wiping her mouth. "But this chicken is the bomb!"

"So, how are you and Maurice doing? Is everything okay?"

"Yeah, I guess," Shaquana said nonchalantly.

She didn't want to let Kenneth know how her man was acting lately. She also didn't want to tell him that she felt that Maurice knew about them being friends, for fear it might run him off. Kenneth sensed the nonchalance, and he knew that she was slowly growing closer to him and pulling away from

Maurice—something unbeknownst to her, yet planned by him.

"So, what's the 'I guess' really mean?" Kenneth asked, emphasizing the word "guess" in air quotes, which made her laugh.

"What?" Kenneth asked, with a smile on his face.

"Ken . . . why you had to pull out quotations?"

"Why you sitting up here acting like we can't talk about anything? Last I checked, we were friends."

"We are, Ken, but what we have has nothing to do with me and my . . . boyfriend," Shaquana said.

What we have! Ken thought, catching her slip. *The heart is something that no man or woman can control.*

"Okay, so tell me about your past boyfriend . . . the one you promised to tell me about," Kenneth said.

"Now that queer homosexual trick we can talk about!" Shaquana said.

"Where is he?"

"Dead!" she told him.

* * *

An hour later, at 11:45 a.m., the duo emerged from the mall, with shopping bags and more food to go.

"So tell me . . . you planned this day, or did it just come to you randomly?" Shaquana asked Kenneth as they walked toward his black Charger embellished with 24-inch dub concave rims and a nice bass system.

"I kinda planned it last night," Kenneth responded as he threw his arms around her neck.

"Thank you, Ken, for bringing me here and buying me these wonderful outfits . . ."

"No need to thank me, Shaquana. We are friends . . . and that's what friend do," Kenneth said.

Neither of them sensed the creeping all-black SUV coming up their backside, with its back window completely down. It was two cars down from Kenneth's Charger when shots were fired, instantly taking down Kenneth to his death. Shaquana dropped everything and scrambled for cover while screaming, with specks of blood from Kenneth's head exploding on her face and chest.

Oh my God! Shaquana thought as she ran deep into the parking lot and hid behind two big vans.

As she looped around the van, she heard two final shots.

Boom! Boom!

She then heard the sound of tires squealing off in escape.

Urrkkkk!

Her heart was racing at one hundred miles per hour, and she was scared like never before. She hid until she heard sirens approaching. Shaquana then ran back to where Kenneth's body was. She just knew he was dead. She had the evidence on her face gathered in tears.

"Nooo! Ken!" Shaquana screamed, covering her mouth with both hands as she collapsed on the ground next to his lifeless body.

He was lying on his stomach with a blank stare and portions of his brains splattered out of his head.

She was back at stage one, realizing that she'd once again lost a good friend in her life.

"He was innocent . . . bastards!" Shaquana cried out in rage as the paramedics and police arrived at the scene.

She was unaware of the crowd that quickly formed around her and began to snap the terrifying, gruesome scenery.

"Damn, lil mama! That's so sad!" D-Rock exclaimed while holding up his iPhone camera among the group.

"Excuse me, ma'am, but we need you to step back out of the way, so we can investigate your boyfriend's death," a female detective said to Shaquana, who was a gorgeous woman who resembled Ice T's wife, Coco.

"Yes, ma'am!" she said as she stood to her feet.

"Would you mind coming with me, ma'am? By the way, my name is Detective Chythia Barns, and we need as much information as we can get to solve your boyfriend's murder . . . beginning with your help," Barns said.

"He was innocent. He did nothing to no one!" Shaquana broke down.

Being accustomed to grieving couples, Detective Barns grabbed Shaquana in a soothing embrace and rubbed her back.

"It's okay, baby. I know your pain from seeing many women in your position. But I promise you that we will find these monsters . . . the killer and the gun that took your boyfriend's life," Barns explained.

* * *

As C-Murder accelerated the stolen black SUV toward the location of the getaway car, Maurice sat on the passenger side with the still-warm .44 Bulldog that he used to kill Kenneth. He was hurt, and badly wanted to take Shaquana to her grave along with Ken. But the love he had for her wouldn't allow him to harm her. He was sure that the loss of her boyfriend would make her suffer extreme grief. Seeing Kenneth's arms around her neck, which led to the ultimate decision to round off on Kenneth, was still in Maurice's head. As C-Murder made a left on Atlanta Boulevard, a tear fell from Maurice's right eye.

Damn! I can't believe this bitch really thought she could play me! Maurice reflected angrily as he wiped the tear away.

C-Murder turned right down a side street and came upon Maurice's Lincoln Navigator.

"Hurry and get to McDonald's. I'm behind you," Maurice said as he hopped out of the stolen SUV and got into his Navigator.

C-Murder accelerated hastily up the road, and Maurice followed behind him en route to the same destination.

"I gotta let that ho go . . . or . . ."

Damn! I can't! Maurice thought, short of speaking what was formulating on his heart, to harm her.

"I can't, Lord! I can't! I love her!" Maurice screamed as the pain he was feeling erupted into tears.

Twenty

When Tameka and D-Zoe pulled up to the mansion in north Miami in a beautiful black limousine, they saw Jean standing outside with four of his men holding M-16 rifles. The limo halted in front of Jean, who Tameka recently had appointed as the head man of her crew. He was no longer a sergeant under Haitian Beny. Jean was now a lieutenant under Tameka, and only a few rules had changed. D-Zoe didn't have to be frisked any longer because now he was her second-in-command.

Jean opened up the back door and reached inside, offering his hand for Tameka to take. She took his massive hand and allowed him to pull her from the confines of the backseat of the limo.

"Welcome, boss lady. Good to see you. We thought it was D-Zoe by himself until we were informed that you would be coming with him," Jean said while kissing Tameka on her hand and treating her like a queen.

Tameka immediately missed the statement about D-Zoe coming by himself, but heard it clearly when he stepped out.

"Never will you see D-Zoe come here without me, Jean. We move together on this side of town . . . understand?" Tameka instructed.

Jean looked at D-Zoe and spoke in Creole to him.

"Is the woman correct? Because we've seen each other twice, and both times you were alone."

The facial expression that appeared on D-Zoe's face told Tameka that there was a problem. But before she could say anything, D-Zoe spoke back to Jean in Creole.

"Do your job as a lieutenant and follow orders. See no evil, hear no evil, speak no evil. That's all you need to be concerned with. You know the code!"

With that said, Jean turned on his heels and walked away mumbling in Creole.

As D-Zoe and Tameka walked into the mansion toward their destination, she reflected on Jean's statement.

Thought that it was D-Zoe himself. . . , she thought.

"D-Zoe . . . you wouldn't happen to come here without my notice to see our guest, would you?" Tameka asked before going inside the room.

"I know the rules, Meka. No, I wouldn't!" he lied.

"Okay, baby! Just checking!" she said, rubbing his face and gently tracing the stitches with her thumb.

"Let's go!" she said as she unlocked the door and walked inside.

When Tameka entered the plush room, she saw that it was completely dark, and being that the room was windowless made it no better. Tameka sensed danger and stopped in her tracks.

This bitch tryin' to play me. I wish she would! Tameka thought as she squatted low and removed her automatic .25 pistol from her thigh holster beneath her Prada dress.

"Champagne!" Tameka called out while pushing the slide back on her small .25.

D-Zoe instinctively had his Glock .19 already out and ready to round off if Champagne had planned an attack.

Who wouldn't in her predicament? he thought as he maneuvered in the darkness by memory in search of the light switch.

When he made it to the switch, he felt a hand. Just as he was about to pull the trigger, he saw Tameka pointing her .25 at him and ready to shoot.

"Boy! You almost got lit up!" Tameka said.

"That makes two of us!" D-Zoe retorted.

When Tameka looked over at the bed, she saw a trembling Champagne tightly holding in her hand what appeared to be a weapon.

"Girl, where do you think you're going to get with that little-ass . . . whatever you call it?" Tameka said as she approached her.

"It ran the last motherfucker off. I'm sure it would get me somewhere," Champagne admitted while watching D-Zoe take a seat in the plush chair in the corner of the room.

When she saw the stitches on his face, she smiled and felt victorious.

"Plus, this little nail, as it is . . . isn't to get me nowhere. It's to protect me from your little rapist!" Champagne informed Tameka, never taking her eyes off of D-Zoe.

She knows! D-Zoe thought as he locked eyes with her.

It's you! You're the rapist! I did that to your face! Champagne realized.

"Champagne . . . what are you telling me? Is someone sexually assaulting you?" Tameka asked with concern, for the last thing she wanted was for someone to be harming her hostage without her say-so.

Champagne looked back at D-Zoe, who was pointing his gun at her and then back at Tameka. He also put his index finger over his mouth to shush her from saying anything.

Champagne was scared and badly wanted to inform Tameka; however, D-Zoe had threatened her life, unbeknownst to Tameka.

Smack!

"Girl! Don't you hear me talking to you?" Tameka screamed after slapping Champagne thunderously, causing her to see stars. "Now, bitch. Answer my question before I take the pussy myself!" Tameka yelled out.

Champagne looked beyond Tameka and saw D-Zoe pointing his gun at her.

"No! There's no one sexually assaulting me. I'm okay. It was just a dream!" Champagne lied.

"Poor baby. You're having nightmares" Tameka asked as she replaced her .25 on her thigh holster and then jumped on the bed with Champagne.

"How would you feel to talk to Jarvis?" Tameka asked her.

Fuck that nigga! Champagne thought.

"I would love to tell him how much a loser he is!" Champagne said.

"Okay!" Tameka said as she looked over at D-Zoe, who was pulling out a TracFone from his jeans.

D-Zoe gently tossed Tameka the phone, and she easily caught it and then dialed Jarvis's number by memory. Tameka then tossed the phone to Champagne, who quickly placed the ringing phone to her ear.

Jarvis was taking a swig from his bottle of Budweiser when his iPhone rang. He reached over, turned down the volume to his flat-screen television, and then answered.

Without looking at the incoming call twice, he knew to whom the unlisted number belonged.

"Hello!" Jarvis answered, getting no immediate reply.

The line was silent for a moment, and then he heard the irrefutable voice of his baby.

"Why Jarvis . . . ?"

"Champagne, baby. Are you okay?" he asked, for he was worried for her well-being but also happy to hear her sweet voice.

"I'm okay, Jarvis. But please tell me, why didn't you leave me on the pole? I would rather strip for the rest of my life than be in trouble because of you . . ."

"Baby, you're coming home . . . !"

"Is that so, Jarvis? Do you have my money?" Tameka asked, snatching the phone out of the hands of Champagne and taking the conversation off speaker.

"Tameka . . . listen! I told you that I have everything now. Just tell me what to do and where to come?" Jarvis asked.

"In two days, I want you to meet me with my men in Palm Beach, just off the Lakeworth exit a mile into town. You'll see a Holiday Inn. Once you're there, I will call you," she explained.

"What's the address of the Holiday Inn . . . ?"

"You'll find it. It's the only one a mile off of the exit," Tameka reiterated and then hung up.

"Shit!" he exclaimed in frustration as he tossed his iPhone onto the side table.

Jarvis had thought about cheating Tameka out of the half billion dollars, but he thought it was too much of a risk. He knew that she was playing five steps ahead of him and that he needed to play by her rules with no cheating.

"Damn, Spin! I need the other half, man!" Jarvis exclaimed, retrieving his phone to call him.

* * *

D-Rock showed up at the trap house in Bankhead thirty minutes after Maurice had pulled up to meet with Coy and C-Murder. They were all looking at the news as well as the footage that D-Rock recorded on his phone.

"Shawty! Look at that, nigga brains! That Bulldog has one hell of a bark!" D-Rock said, pointing at the scene on his phone screen.

"Now look at this!" D-Rock continued, sliding his thumb across the screen and pulling up another gruesome scene of Kenneth's baby mama slain.

"Damn, D-Rock! You and Coy did a number, huh?" Maurice said as he stared at the screen of Trish's dead body.

"Where was the baby girl?" Maurice asked.

"Fortunately, the baby was with her Grams . . . just like I preferred it to be. I hate doing kids, cuzo!" D-Rock said.

"Yo, Mauri! Check this shit out!" Coy announced while turning up the volume on the television, revealing footage of Daquan sitting at a table with his lawyer, Mr. Goodman.

"Today, Daquan Coleman Clark stepped into the 3rd Circuit Court of Jonesboro with his attorneys, Mr. Goodman and Ms. McKnight. They presented to Judge Kenny Stuart a motion to suppress the murder weapon in this case, for it was obtained illegally. Let's go inside the courtroom and find out what seems to have prosecutor Matthew Brooks on edge."

Brooks: "Your Honor . . . I would like to object to this motion on the formal grounds of statute 323.016, which states that the law has a right to execute for probable cause . . ."

Goodman: "Your Honor . . . 323.016 translates exactly how he's saying, but we're not arguing the formal statute. It is clear that the defendant's rights have been violated, sir, from points A to C. You can clearly see that the defendant had invoked his right to remain silent. So if there was any reinitiation, there still had to be a lawyer present as stated in Statute 300.217, sir."

Judge Stuart: "The tape has been reviewed by the state, and it clearly shows that the detectives violated his rights . . . I grant the defense's motion."

"I'll be damned!" Maurice exclaimed in shock.

"Listen! Listen! There's more!" Coy shouted.

"People . . . we've just seen Judge Stuart throw out the murder weapon in Daquan Coleman Clark's case, where he also has a codefendant named Thorton Petway, who is being housed separately from Mr. Clark. The state is completely devastated by this move because now it makes their case feeble against Mr. Clark and Petway. I'm Melissa Anderson reporting live from the Jonesboro courthouse. And now we would like to go to a breaking news update in Atlanta," the sexy blonde reporter stated.

"We're live still on the scene at the Lenox Mall in Atlanta where a gruesome murder is still being investigated. The victim's name is now being released as Kenneth Humphrey, who was a student at adult-aid education, striving to become a law enforcement officer along with his girlfriend, who we see in the background crying hysterically . . . ," the report continued.

"He was innocent. He did nothing wrong!" Shaquana screamed, unaware that she was live on the news.

Maurice couldn't take seeing his woman cry out for another man, so he stormed out from the living room and house altogether. He hopped into his Escalade and accelerated to Jonesboro. He was tired of holding back. What he had on his mind wasn't getting her back; it was following his heart. He didn't know how to approach the situation. He just knew that after seeing Shaquana's heart destroyed because of another man's death—a man that she'd been cheating on him with—that there was nothing restraining him from what he had in mind to do to her. It was something he wanted to do for a long time, and now he had the opportunity to do so.

* * *

Tittyboo was the happiest man in the dormitory after seeing—with his own eyes—the state's loss against Daquan.

"His win was a win for me because they were charging both of us!" he constantly reminded himself.

Tittyboo had a visit with his lawyer, who was just as elated with the news. Mrs. Brown had informed him to stay away from friends in jail because an informant was bound to come in his direction. However, unbeknownst to them both, Barns was already five moves ahead of the judge's decision in favor of the defense.

He cried silent tears of joy alone in his cell as he looked forward to his soon-to-be freedom.

"Soon, man, I'll be home!" he said while wiping away the tears falling from his eyes.

* * *

Brenda had just watched the news and was now on the phone with a grieving Shaquana, when she heard a knock on her door.

"Baby, you just got to tell him about it and see where things go from there. If I seen it, the whole damn state of Georgia did . . ."

Knock! Knock! Knock!

"I'm coming!" she yelled out as she made her way to the door while still in conversation with Shaquana. "Meantime, I'ma go see Daquan today and see what's next. Call me when . . ." Brenda choked up on her statement as she opened the door and saw her visitor. He was handsome and had pain written all over his face as the tears fell from his eyes unabashed.

"Baby, I will call you . . . !"

Brenda was cut off short as he grabbed the back of her neck vigorously and placed his mouth to hers. He kissed her deeply and passionately while backing her into her home and closing the door.

With the phone still in her hand, Brenda disconnected the phone call, put her arms around her visitor, and wrapped her legs around his waist. She roughly kissed him while caressing his face.

"To the room, baby!" Brenda moaned out as he carried her upstairs in his strong arms.

Once inside the bedroom, he pulled off his black wifebeater and pants and then helped her out of her black tights and bra. He slowly removed her sexy satin lingerie with his mouth and then buried his face into her sultry mound. She arched her back as he sucked on her throbbing clitoris and called out his name: "Maurice!"

It was far from a dream, and she didn't want it to end. Her body began to tremble as she came to her climax.

"Uhhh!" she moaned as her creamy flow fell into Maurice's mouth. He slurped her creamy surge and then swiped his tongue across her asshole.

"Oh my God, Maurice! Please fuck me now!" Brenda yelled, begging for his thrust.

"Anything at your behest, baby!" Maurice retorted as he took off his briefs and climbed on top of her as she spread her legs wide like an eagle and allowed him to enter her.

"Uhhh! Shit!" Brenda moaned out as Maurice filled up her womb with his length.

He handled her gently and made every stroke of his thrusting send an electrifying climax throughout her body. When she looked into Maurice's eyes, she saw so much pain from a heart being broken. His salty tears fell from his eyes and dripped on her face. She knew what he was experiencing and could share the same pain because she knew what it felt like to hurt a man. She had no regrets and vowed to never hurt him like she hurt Jerome.

Brenda clamped down on him and brought his painful face to hers and spoke truthfully to him.

"I'm here for you, baby. No more pain!"

Twenty-One

"Shaquana . . . how long have you known Kenneth?" Detective Barns asked while the two of them were sitting at an interrogation table at the Atlanta precinct.

"I've only known him a few months," she replied, wiping her eyes with a tissue.

She tried calling Maurice to explain, but he wasn't answering his phone. The entire state of Georgia knew about the mall shooting, and things only got worse when Kenneth's baby's mother, Trish, was found slain in her apartment.

"How was your boyfriend feeling about you and Kenneth's friendship? Was there any type of disapproval?" Barns asked.

Damn! Could Maurice have done this? No way! He was in court with Daquan. But that doesn't mean he couldn't pay someone else to do it! Shaquana thought.

"Ma'am, we need to know everything. Is it possible that your boyfriend could have done this to Kenneth out of . . . ?"

"There's no way he could have done it. He was in court with my brother," Shaquana said confidently.

"Okay, so he's okay with you and Kenneth's relationship?" Barns pressed on.

"Miss . . . me and Kenneth were only classmates . . ."

"That's not what I'm hearing. In fact, we've pulled the tapes. You two seemed very romantic," Barns added.

"Miss . . . listen. I've had enough for one day. Can I leave? I no longer want to be here!" Shaquana said.

"Of course you can leave, Shaquana. Just know that we will be in contact and that you'll probably see more of me. Please expect us to make a visit to your boyfriend, Mr. Maurice Holmes, who definitely wasn't in court like you've stated," Detective Chythia Barns said as she quickly walked out of the room, leaving Shaquana with her thoughts and free to leave.

The feeling that overcame her left her confused and scared to face the man she loved—and almost fell out of love with for a man who was now dead.

Did Maurice kill him? she thought.

* * *

"Yes, daddy!" Tameka purred as Cuban Black penetrated her deeply and rapidly while she was balled into a pretzel on the queen-size bed at her beach house.

She had finally gotten him to come to her place, where she prepared a delicious dinner for him and then gave him a relaxing massage in her hot tub. There was something about Cuban Black that made her yearn for him more and more every day. Despite her self-commitment to not fall deeply for a man, after what Jarvis had done to her, she found herself falling for Cuban Black. However, it scared her because he too, like Benjamin, was a married man, which meant that he wouldn't be completely hers.

She tried to convince herself that it was only sex that she was concerned with and nothing serious. But it was hard when Cuban Black was actually making rough love to her and making her feel special. Tameka then came to another volatile orgasm, followed by Cuban Black exploding inside of her.

"Arrgghhh! Shit, baby!" he groaned as he continued to shoot his load inside her tight pussy.

"Uhh . . . uhh . . . uhh!" Tameka screamed, all sweaty, over-climaxed, and exhausted.

Cuban Black slowly unwove Tameka from her pretzel position while massaging her caramel stallion thighs to soothe any discomfort.

"I bet you a million dollars that you can't walk to that bathroom or . . . better yet . . . to the kitchen to grab daddy something to drink," he said breathlessly.

"And I bet you'll go get it before me!" she retorted while rubbing his muscular arms.

"Oh yeah?" Cuban Black said, with his right eye jacked up like the WWE wrestler/actor The Rock.

"Yeah, daddy. Can you please fix me a glass of water? Pleeeease!" Tameka joked seductively.

"Oh, so that's how you're going to get it, huh?"

"Wouldn't you agree that I deserve it?" Tameka asked Cuban Black, cutting him off as he continued to massage and outstretch her thighs.

"You win . . . only because I can't tell you no!" he said as he pulled on his pair of Polo briefs.

Before he walked out of the room, he looked back at Tameka—whose eyes were locked in on him—and asked, "Can you get used to this?"

"To you?" she asked, a bit perplexed.

"To everything?" Cuban Black retorted.

"Of course, I can. It wasn't planned, and despite the small issues, I know that we could work around them," Tameka said, talking about his three wives.

"That's why I like you, beautiful . . ."

"And Victor . . . I can't explain to you how I feel, but I'm sure it's the same feelings as yours," she added.

"How can you be sure of that?" he asked.

"I wouldn't be splitting half a billion dollars with you if it wasn't!" she answered back.

It was all Cuban Black needed to hear. He turned on his heels and proceeded to go get his partner a glass of water. Tameka had come to the finality of splitting half a billion dollars with him, and for him to give her the ownership of some of his establishments.

Cuban Black was the epitome of a real business man, who the feds desperately could not figure out. And that's the team Tameka wanted to be on—as his partner, lover, and friend.

As Tameka sat up in the bed and waited for Cuban Black to return, her mind just couldn't stay off of the half billion dollars. She had wracked her nerves trying to figure out how Jarvis had come up with the money. It was preposterous, and she couldn't fathom how any small million-dollar drug dealer could accumulate that amount of cash so easily.

I swear, if he's playing me, I will kill him and his girlfriend! Tameka thought.

If not for Cuban Black, Tameka would have delivered Champagne to Jarvis in a box and then taken his life as well. But Cuban Black explained to her to keep everything on the up and up. He then gave her a speech about how he had reached the top by being fair in business.

Damn! This man is truly one of a kind! she considered, with a content smile on her face. *What's going on with me? Am I falling for him; and if I am, would . . .*

Boc! Boc! Boc!

"What the fuck!" Tameka screamed as she heard the shots close by outside.

She quickly leaped from the bed and killed all the lights in the room.

Boc! Boc! Boc!

The shots continued as she reached into her bottom nightstand drawer to retrieve her fully automatic Glock .21. Tameka quickly slid into a silk robe and exited her room with the Glock in her hands at a ready position.

Boc! Boc! Boc!

As she neared the corner that led into the kitchen, Cuban black grabbed her from behind and snatched her back into the hall, causing her to pull the trigger twice, startling her to death.

Boc! Boc!

As she tried to yell for Cuban Black, his hands wrapped around her mouth, muffling her screams.

"It's me, baby! Calm down!" Cuban Black whispered in her ear.

At the sound of his voice, Tameka immediately calmed down and then turned around to see that Cuban Black was holding a big .357 snub nose in his hand.

"Baby! What's going on?" she asked Cuban Black, who appeared to be very calm.

"Never panic, baby!" he told her as the shots ceased outside.

"My men are handling the situation well . . ."

"What men? You didn't tell me that you had men outside, Victor!"

"And I'll never go anywhere without them. I'm not naive

to those who want Cuban Black dead and out of the way. Now, let me go see what's going on. Stay here . . . !"

"No! I'm coming with you," Tameka said adamantly.

A scowl appeared on Cuban Black's face for a moment, until he realized who he was dealing with. As badly as he wanted to protect her, he knew her courage was what most men lacked.

"Come, but keep close by . . . and keep your eyes open."

"I will. I promise," she responded.

Tameka walked outside behind Cuban Black, with her weapon held in a firm grip. When Cuban Black walked out into the parking lot, he saw that the driver's side of his limo door was partially opened, with the driver's leg hanging out. He knew from the position and the way the leg stuck out that his driver, Ted, was dead.

Excessive bullet holes pierced the limo's exterior.

"Damn it!" Cuban Black exclaimed as he opened the door and found a lifeless Ted slumped across the seat.

When he began to look around, Tameka knew by the look on his face that he was looking for other bodies.

Where the fuck are Mat and Jimbo? he thought of his two professional bodyguards.

"What's wrong, baby?" Tameka asked as nearby sirens could be heard.

Cuban Black looked around until he saw the dark pathway leading up alongside her house.

"Come, baby. Now!" he said as they made a dash to the side of the house.

He halted when he saw a figure lying on the ramp that led out toward the beach. Cuban Black quickly ran toward the figure and knelt down to find Jimbo, still breathing while lying on his back.

"Damn it, man. What happened?"

Jimbo was slowly dying, with bubbles of blood pouring from his mouth.

"He came up by the . . . beach. He knows her," Jimbo said in severe pain. "He chased Mat on the beach. I tried . . ."

"You did good, Jimbo. You hear me, huh?"

Jimbo took his last breath and could not answer back.

"Damn it, man!" Cuban Black exclaimed as he made a dash down to the beach where he stumbled upon Mat, who was like the rest of his men—dead.

"Damn, baby! Who could have done this shit?" Cuban Black asked Tameka, who was as stunned at the revelation as he was hurt by losing his long-term men.

"I have no clue, baby!"

"Who wants you bad enough to spy on you, Meka? Think!" Cuban Black exclaimed angrily as he grabbed her by her face and looked into her eyes.

The look he had in his burning eyes told a story that she had yet to hear him tell her. Tameka was unable to hold the stare, so she closed her eyes and thought for a moment.

D-Zoe! she thought.

He was obsessed with her, and the only name that came to her mind. But she would not bring his name out of her mouth, because she knew that it would be signing his death sentence.

"Baby! I don't know who could have done this!"

Cuban Black searched her eyes for any sign of dishonesty, but he could find none.

"We have to go, Meka. We can't be here when the police come. Let's go!" Cuban Black said, grabbing her by her hand and then taking off in another dash further down the beach to get as far away from the crime scene as possible.

* * *

D-Zoe had made it down the beach and then come upon another beach house. Fortunately, no one was home, so he maneuvered inconspicuously through the darkness. When he came back into view of South Beach, he quickly hailed a cab and drove away from the scene with no further problems.

As the cab driver accelerated to his destination, D-Zoe thought about Tameka's whorish ways. He had watched her and Cuban Black the entire night, and he came to kill them both, but he was interrupted by Cuban Black's bodyguards that he had to put down.

They ruined my intentions of killing the grimy bitch and her lover! D-Zoe thought angrily. *But I will have the both of them. She thinks she can play with a man's heart!* D-Zoe reflected with frustration.

"Change of plans. Take me to Club King of Diamond," D-Zoe told the Arab driver.

"Yes, sir!" the driver answered.

D-Zoe wanted to get some drink in his system and look for a nice-looking stripper that he could take out his sexual frustrations on willingly—and unwillingly.

Twenty-Two

Shaquana was sitting in front of the flat screen television in the living room of their suite when Maurice finally walked through the door. It was 3:45 a.m., and despite her guilt and exhaustion, she had questions for him coming in so late.

As he looked at her sitting with both her feet underneath her, Maurice badly wanted to go grab her and embrace her. But her betrayal wouldn't allow him to be compassionate.

Maurice had nothing to say as he attempted to storm into the room, but he was stopped short when Shaquana made a quick dash and blocked his way.

"Maurice, please! Listen to me! I know the thoughts that are going through your head. But I can explain . . . !"

"Explain what, huh?" Maurice screamed out to Shaquana while going through the gallery in his iPhone. "Explain day one, Shaquana!"

Maurice presented a slide show of her and Kenneth hanging out, beginning with the first day when she gave him a ride home.

Oh my God! How did he see me? I can't remember him being in my sight, she pondered.

"What? You think I'm stupid? Then you sitting up here crying for the bastard, huh?" Maurice continued to scream out in rage.

He was hurt, and it was evident to Shaquana. But she had no intentions of hurting her man.

But damn, Mauri! It's not what it looks like, Shaquana thought.

"Baby! It's not what you think!" she said as she reached out to grab him.

But she was pushed away so vigorously that she fell to the ground and hit her head.

"Aww!"

"It's not what I'm thinking, huh? Haven't I heard that over and over?" Maurice yelled out while standing over her.

"Maurice . . . he was a friend and not what you think!" Shaquana screamed, with tears cascading down her face.

"Friend, huh? What is that?" Maurice asked her as he threw the phone at her, hitting her in the face.

"Maurice!" she cried out.

She couldn't believe how he was treating her, but she expected nothing else.

"Look at the damn phone, 'Quana!" he barked.

When she looked at the phone with trembling hands, her head felt like it was about to explode. She was looking at her last time with Kenneth, just moments before he was killed.

Maurice killed Ken! Shaquana admitted to herself.

She had nothing to say to him that could explain the intimacy level between her and Ken that was being displayed.

"Maurice! You don't understand . . . !"

"Understand what 'Quana, huh? You cheated on me, and for what . . . just because he wanted to be in the police, too?"

"No, Maurice. I didn't . . ."

"Save that shit, 'Quana, for a busta. Just know this . . . if I didn't love you, I would have shot you down as you ran away toward the big vans. The bullets were meant for two, but the heart only spoke up for one," Maurice said as he snatched away his iPhone from her hands.

"Maurice . . . I'm sorry, please!" she cried out as she ran after her man, who was attempting to leave the suite.

He then stopped in his tracks and turned around to face Shaquana.

"Please what, 'Quana? Love you? I did that. Don't cheat on you? I did that too, until recently. You were having fun, so I did the same thing, and I enjoyed every unregretful moment of it. I don't have shit to say to you. Being that your friend is now stiff, I'ma give you time to yourself to grieve . . ."

"Maurice, please! I love you, and I did not cheat on you. I was just . . ."

"You still in denial. 'Quana . . . take your time. Yes, we are going through some things at the moment. But I have faith that we'll work it out. Just not anytime soon," he told her before storming off.

When he was gone, Shaquana cried like never before. She cried for both men—one man who she hurt and one man who was dead because she hid him from her man.

He was just a friend, Mauri. Why did you have to kill him . . . and his baby mama? Shaquana thought, realizing at that moment how cruel her man was.

The pictures he showed Shaquana left no doubt in her mind that Maurice had killed Kenneth.

How could I be in love with such a cold-blooded animal? she questioned herself introspectively.

It wasn't like she wasn't accustomed to seeing murder. Her dad had plenty of men killed, and her brother was facing a murder case himself. What bothered Shaquana was that she only wanted death to occur to the ones who killed her father and mother.

He killed Kenneth . . . and he killed him for all the wrong reasons. It is my fault that Ken is dead. I shouldn't have hid him, because it looked like we were more than friends, Shaquana thought as she viewed the prospect of her and Ken from any man's perspective.

She knew that she hurt her man, and it was shown by the pain in his face. She loved Maurice and wanted him to know the truth of her and Ken.

"Was I falling for Ken?" she asked herself as she replayed all the good times they had together—all the lunches and morning breakfasts they shared that Maurice witnessed.

"Damn!" Shaquana exclaimed, realizing that she had made a big mistake.

She wiped her eyes and then sat down on the plush leather sofa and stared at the picture of her best friend, Champagne, on the news. Shaquana grabbed the remote and turned up the volume on the TV: "We're still asking for any helpful information that could lead to any clues about the disappearance of Champagne Robinson. Please contact the Jonesboro Police Department at 800-216-3722."

Shaquana turned off the television and sat in complete darkness. She had to find a way to get Maurice to understand her. Despite everything he revealed, the only thing that now stuck in her conscience was that he had admitted to cheating on her.

I knew he was seeing someone else. He thinks I cheated on him, so he's been lying up with another woman. I swear, I will kill her and him. But how can I blame him, and how can

I get upset? What man would have seen it differently? Shaquana thought considerately.

"Maurice . . . I love you, and I will not let another woman love you. I'm sorry!" Shaquana yelled out before she cried herself to sleep.

* * *

At the Barnses' residence, Lieutenant Chythia Barns lay in her husband's arms after pleasing him with her sweet, passionate loving. She had to have him inside her at least two times a day to be content.

It was almost 5:00 a.m., which meant that both of them soon had to rise and get ready for their daily jobs as detectives. She was a lieutenant detective, and he was a sergeant detective, and they both had highly regarded reputations as superb detectives.

Chythia sat in silence while rubbing her husband's hairy chest and stomach. She could tell that he was bothered by the weak performance he gave during sex, but she decided to work with him instead of chastising him.

"When I was a stripper, you were able to pull me to the side and show me my worth as a woman. When I was down . . . when my mother passed away . . . it was you, Danny, who consoled me and cared for me," Chythia said. "What's wrong, Danny?" she asked when she saw her husband let out a sigh.

"That boy killed that girl and had his friend's girlfriend assassinated. I can't believe Judge Stuart dismissed the murder weapon!" he explained.

Chythia knew that the judge's decision had upset her husband from the moment she heard the news. Every time she would think about Daquan, her past with his father came up.

Daquan could have been my burden, she thought in retrospection about when Benjamin and she were expecting a child before she met her husband.

She never told him of her fling with Benjamin and her miscarriage. And she also never told her husband of her true feelings for Benjamin. In fact, when she saw Shaquana, she badly wanted to let her know why her dedication to help her was so intense. But she kept it professional and vowed to catch the killer, starting with her boyfriend.

"Listen, baby!" Chythia said, climbing on top of her husband and looking into his stress-filled eyes.

Damn! He's aging, she thought to herself as she paid close attention to the excessive gray hair overtaking his dark brown hair.

"The judge did what he felt was fair. Don't beat yourself up. You have confidential informants, and you have him on tape."

"The tape's not presented yet until we give Joshah a deal, and they're warrantless . . ."

"Why aren't there any warrants for the tapes, Danny? You know you can't be going over the law's head . . . at least not all the time!" Chythia explained.

"I know. But without the weapon, he walks," Barns sadly said to his wife.

"Listen!" she said, grabbing him by his chin and forcing him to look into her eyes.

"Don't let this beat you down. You are the Bulldog, remember that! We will make sure that Daquan Clark goes to the gas chamber by all means . . . ," she said before getting quiet. "Even if I have to fuck the damn judge myself!" she added, just to make Danny feel good and get a good laugh out of him.

"Woman! You're cold. I will not let the judge sample my goodies . . ."

"Then get it together, honey!" Chythia retorted.

"I will. I promise!" Detective Danny Barns exclaimed as he positioned himself inside of Chythia's still-moist pussy, ramming all of his length inside her.

"Awww! Now that's my Danny!" she purred, loving the feel of him deep inside her.

She rode him wild until the break of dawn, where they both prepared themselves for another long day of work. He was going after Daquan Coleman Clark, and she was pursuing Maurice Dean Holmes. Both of the Barnses hadn't the slightest clue of the inevitable danger that came with seeking two powerful suspects.

* * * * *

When Maurice opened his eyes from his cat nap, he saw Brenda bringing him breakfast on a silver platter.

"Damn! Breakfast in bed, huh?" Maurice exclaimed.

"Yep! And you're not dreaming!" she said as she laid the platter on Maurice's lap and then walked back out of the room.

As she strutted away, Maurice stared at her lustfully, as he was ready to pounce on her again. She was wearing a T-shirt and satin thong that was being swallowed up by her delicate curves.

Damn! That woman knows she's gorgeous! Maurice thought as he admired her scintillating beauty.

When Brenda came back, she was carrying two glasses of orange juice. She set them both down on the nightstand closer to Maurice, and then climbed into bed with him and began stirring his steaming cheesy grits.

"Open, baby!" Brenda said as she stuffed a spoonful of grits into Maurice's mouth.

"Yumm! Delicious!" he closed his eyes and said.

"That's an insult. It's the bomb, negro!" Brenda retorted.

"Sorry! It's the bomb!" Maurice followed.

For the next twenty minutes, Brenda fed Maurice and then once again rode him slowly and passionately. She made sweet love to him, taking her time with him and dragging him deeper into her world.

I'm not going to lose this one, Lord, Brenda thought as she slowly rode Maurice's love tool to her climax.

Twenty-Three

Joshah walked out of the Jonesboro jail a happy man. He was free, despite the deal he agreed to, to follow up for the state and testify against Daquan.

"These crackers done fucked up and let the boy out," Joshah exclaimed as he walked to the nearest payphone and dialed Detective Barns's number.

Barns picked up on the second ring and spoke. "Detective Barns here. I'm guessing this is Joshah."

Dumb-ass cracker. You know this me! Joshah thought.

"Yeah, I'm out and waiting on you," Joshah said.

"Walk down the main road, and I'll be there shortly."

"It's almost over with, shawty. Bad as I want to beat Daquan's ass, I'll never role on the other side. I'll die before I turn state," Joshah said as he walked toward the main road.

He knew that the tape of him recording Daquan in the cell would be useless if he didn't testify, and Joshah had no strong intentions of taking the stand. He was only focused on his own freedom and getting out of town, once he found his alleged rapid victim and finished her off.

A half mile down the road, Joshah was hot and covered in sweat. Barns pulled behind him in an unmarked black SUV and let the window down.

"Come on, son, and let me give you a lift," Detective Barns exclaimed as he unlocked the passenger door.

"Damn! I thought you said you'll be here shortly. I've been walking this hot-ass road more than shortly," Joshah said.

"Get in before I change my mind and have your ass thrown back in jail . . . since you're already impatient," Barns followed up.

Cracker! The last thing you'll want to do is put me back in jail! Joshah thought as he got into the SUV.

"So are you ready for this?" Barns asked.

"If I wasn't, I wouldn't be here!" he retorted.

* * *

Jarvis was on the road heading south to Florida in his new Lincoln Navigator. In the backseat, hidden in a secret compartment, was half of what Spin had given him in counterfeit bills. Jarvis had spoken with him and was happy to hear that Spin had the other half. Emanating from his speakers was an old-school hit by Easy-E. Jarvis was eager to get to Jacksonville to meet up with Spin and then be on his way to Palm Beach.

It's almost over, baby! Jarvis thought to himself.

"Approximately one hour and thirty minutes until you reach Jacksonville, Florida. Keep straight," the GPS system announced over Jarvis's Bluetooth.

"One hour, baby. Let's go!" he exclaimed ecstatically while rubbing his hands together as if he was trying to keep warm.

Despite his anxiousness, Jarvis was aware that when he arrived in Palm Beach, things could go wrong, so he was prepared and was fully equipped with plenty of firepower. Jarvis wasn't going down without a fight, and he didn't plan on leaving Palm Beach without Champagne. As he accelerated gingerly to avoid state trooper traps, his mind was on his reunion with Champagne. He was so locked in on the thoughts of the two of them that he never noticed the FBI on his trail.

* * *

When Daquan walked into the attorney-client room, he saw his lawyer, Mr. Goodman, sitting alone at the table, with an unpleasant look on his face. He immediately realized that something was wrong.

What's the scowl for? Daquan thought as he sat down at the table.

He noticed that Goodman had another large manila envelope in his possession. Daquan was still in isolation for his fight with Joshah, and had a month to go until his time was up and he was allowed to return to open population. It sucked because he couldn't receive any personal visits, but he managed to get through.

"How are you doing, Daquan?" Goodman asked nonchalantly.

Something's up, because that don't even sound like Goodman, Daquan thought before he spoke.

"I'm okay. Do we have a date?"

"Son, listen. Let's not move too fast. We have some serious problems . . ."

"What do you mean serious problems?" Daquan inquired skeptically.

"Daquan . . . you're never supposed to engage in talk with anyone about your case . . ."

Damn! Daquan thought as he instantly felt a stomach full of butterflies.

"Check this shit out!" Goodman said, removing the contents of the manila envelope and sliding them over to Daquan. "There are five tape recordings that your last cellmate has of you and him conversing about your case, including the night you beat the shit out of him. So I'm guessing he's more eager about taking the stand against you now . . . !"

"Ain't this shit illegal? He can't record me without a warrant and me being aware. I've seen it in the law library," Daquan exclaimed, recalling the many cases he had read about on illegal wiring.

"Kid, I like your wits. Yes! It's illegal, but only if it's reversed on appeal, son, and we're not trying to see an appeal. We're trying to knock this ball out of the park!" Goodman said to him with emphasis.

"So, what do this mean?"

"It only means more work. Mr. Brooks was happy to hand me over another supplement to your case. Just from here on out, Daquan, please speak to no one about your case. If anybody asks, beat their ass because nine times out of ten, they're the motherfucking police."

Daquan liked how his lawyer gave it to him like a straight ol' G would. It wouldn't be wise to underestimate Goodman by his costly suits and Keith Sweat talk, because he would bring the hood out in a minute. He was the type of ol' G who never left the hood. He just knew how to control the hood and not let the hood take control of him.

"I got you, sir!" Daquan responded.

"Okay. Next . . . we have a scheduled court date next month . . ."

"Next month, really? It's going forward? I thought he would drop the case . . . !"

"Son, with shit like this?" Goodman said, pointing at the document of Joshah's recordings lying on the table.

"Hell, I'd be eager to try my luck if I was him too," Goodman said.

I can't believe this snake-ass nigga Joshah. I knew there was something stank about that nigga. Damn! How did I slip? Daquan contemplated.

"Where is Joshah now?" Daquan inquired.

"I thought you'd never ask! Joshah was released, and his rape charge has been removed. But we know that it won't be official until after he takes the stand against you," Goodman said.

Damn it! Daquan thought with frustration.

"I need your help, Mr. Goodman."

"I'm here. What is it that you need, son?" Goodman asked.

"I need to know where I can find him."

Mr. Goodman looked at Daquan with a smirk on his face, realizing exactly what Daquan's intentions were. On another day, Goodman would have told him that he was out of his mind, but Goodman himself had pressure to win Daquan's case. Goodman was down for anything that would help him win—even cheating.

I can't let Brenda expose the sex tape, for it would ruin my life in a rapid domino effect, taking my wife, money, job, and possibly my life. For who would want to live after losing a career and family because of a fucking sex tape? Goodman thought. *Everything Daquan needs me to do . . . all but pull a trigger. I have no choice but to do it!*

"Daquan, I'll mail you his location. Once you get it, for both our sakes, please destroy it!" Mr. Goodman told him.

"I will, sir. I promise!" Daquan retorted, with a bright smile on his face.

* * *

"So, you feel Mauri killed Kenneth just because he showed you some pictures?" Brenda asked Shaquana, who was being adamant about accusing Maurice of the murder of Kenneth.

Shaquana had come over to Brenda's house after school because she had no interest in going straight home and she needed to talk to someone about what was heavy on her chest. Brenda had texted Maurice an hour before to inform him that Shaquana was at her house, to prevent any suspicions if he showed up while Shaquana was sitting in her living room. Because the last thing Brenda needed was Shaquana's instinct to cause her to snoop around and ruin her fling with Maurice, who was in her bed every night at a reasonable time.

"Baby, listen. All I'm saying is to never jump to any conclusions. We know Mauri . . ."

Why the fuck is she calling him Mauri like that? Shaquana wondered, irked.

"We know he'll lay a nigga down. If you stop worrying about a man who's gone and see about patching up your relationship, Shaquana, none of that would matter . . ."

"Auntie Brenda . . . Ken didn't deserve to die. I love Maurice too much to cheat on him . . ."

"But, Shaquana, you can't see the pain he was in when you hid him from Ken . . . and Ken from Maurice. Your mistake only got a man killed because that man loved you."

She's right! Shaquana realized. *He told me that he could have killed me, and he could have, but . . . he loved me, and I hurt him. I caused him to go out and cheat.*

"Baby, give him some time to heal. Don't stress yourself. Just let him cool down, and when he do, explain everything to him," Brenda advised.

"He's sleeping with someone else. He told me! He really . . ."

"Shaquana . . . so what! Do you blame him? Let's wear his shoes. Wouldn't you find you a sidekick if you felt he had one? Love is something you two have, and a piece of pussy can't amount to what you two have. Don't worry about no call girl!" Brenda said, regretting the words coming from her mouth because they seemed to go for her as well.

Practice what you preach, sista! Brenda thought.

"I'm a wait until he comes home and ready to talk, Auntie," Shaquana finally concluded.

The rest of the night the twosome watched Jerome play in his first NFL game as a Cowboy linebacker against the Miami Dolphins. The score was a blowout at 21-0, and Jerome was already starting his rookie season with forced fumbles.

After Shaquana left, Maurice pulled in an hour later and finished watching the fourth quarter with Brenda. When the question had come back to the surface of what really happened in her and Jerome's relationship, Brenda broke down emotionally and came out clean with Maurice. He held her, kissed her tears away, and made love to her,

193

understanding her indelible pain. Despite being furious, Maurice understood her intentions.

"Never again will you have to give up something so precious!" Maurice whispered in her ear as he held her in his arms while lying on the plush sofa. Together, exhausted and sweaty, the twosome fell asleep comfortably.

* * *

Jarvis couldn't believe how Spin had him waiting all day. Every hour was an excuse, and Jarvis was beginning to get skeptical. He was impatiently waiting at a cheap, filthy motel on the outskirts of Jacksonville's gutters.

"This motherfucker gonna make me whack his ass when I do see him!" Jarvis exclaimed while pacing the small one-bed motel room.

From time to time, Jarvis would look out and survey the post-midnight atmosphere, playing the darkness to his advantage. As he was watching, he saw a black SUV pull into the small parking lot and loop around in a circle. He paid close attention to it as it came to a halt across from his Navigator. He watched the lights die, and then all the doors opened at once. Four men stepped out, who were the size of club bouncers, standing as giants at six foot five and 300 pounds.

"Who the fuck are these motherfuckers!" Jarvis said to himself as his iPhone rang.

When he looked at the caller, he saw that it was Spin again.

"Please tell me we're not still busy, man. It's three o'clock in the morning! I'm like twelve hours late for a date!"

Jarvis said into the phone to Spin.

"I'm sorry, son. But it's been a hard day for me. I had to wait on my connect to bring everything to me from a twelve-hour drive himself. Once again, my apology is genuinely sincere . . ."

"So are we ready, because I really need to be on my way?" Jarvis asked.

"Of course we are ready. The four men standing outside are with me. I'm inside the truck. Come and let me have a short word with you . . ."

Damn! Something smells like fish! Jarvis thought instinctively.

He had a bad feeling about everything, but he had to test the waters, for he badly needed the other half of his deal.

"I'm coming, man, Spin. I can't stay for long, shawty. I'm seriously running behind on time to being at my destination," Jarvis said.

"Jarvis . . . I could fly you to your destination, and I'm not being all talk. I'm serious, son! Since I've held you up all day, I'm offering you that chance," Spin said sincerely.

"Maybe I could use a lift in the air, Spin!" Jarvis said.

"Well, hurry. Let's get our business over with so that we all can be on our way," Spin replied.

"Okay! I'm coming now," Jarvis said as he disconnected the call.

Looking around in the darkness, Jarvis walked to the bed and felt for his tools. He cocked back both Glock .21s and tucked them into his front waistband, and he put on his black leather jacket. He would bypass all pat downs if there were any, and would be adamant about giving up his tools without a fight.

There are too many against one out-of-town-ass nigga. I won't hesitate to blow any of them giants away! Jarvis thought as he stepped outside and walked toward the SUV with the four bouncers hanging outside.

He spotted Big Shawn among them, which brought the stranger count down to three.

"What's up, Big Shawn?" Jarvis said as he came near.

"Everything cool. The man is inside waiting on you. I don't want to frustrate you anymore than you are, but I can't allow you to go inside if you're holding, Jarvis, and you'll have to be patted down . . ."

"Big Shawn . . . you know I'm holding, and the last thing I will do is give up my tools. If I can't step in with my shit, then tell him to come out here and talk to me," Jarvis exclaimed.

For a moment, there was an eerie silence among them all.

I know this nigga ain't trying to play me! he thought.

"Jarvis, we can do this the hard way or . . ."

Before Big Shawn could get the words out, Jarvis stunned them all with his agility as he pulled out both Glock .21s and took out two men in no time, sending muffled shots into their throats.

The silencers kicked off like a mad snake hissing. Big Shawn tried getting to his Mac-10 and was stopped short as two bullets pierced his shoulders and spun him around.

Jarvis rounded off at the last man, who had difficulties serving his duty from fumbling with his Glock .19. Jarvis put one in his neck and a few in his chest, turning his world from red to dark.

"Tell me why I shouldn't kill your ass, nigga!" Jarvis asked Big Shawn, who stood defenseless with both shoulders wounded and in pain. He was panting and looked like he was on the verge of passing out.

"Man . . . we just trying to protect our man, Jarvis!" Big Shawn said breathlessly.

Jarvis aimed at Big Shawn's head and then looked at the back door of the SUV. He was taking a chance with Spin, not knowing if he himself was under the scope of a gun.

"Come out, Spin, or I will take him like the rest!" Jarvis demanded.

In no time, Spin opened the back door and emerged fearless while smoking on a kush blunt twisted from a Dutch cigar.

"Damn, Jarvis! You killed all my men. What is this about?"

"Don't play me, Spin. You niggas came out here with the games. You should have known not to play me . . . asking me for my tools," Jarvis said before he began to chuckle. "What you niggas take me for, huh?" he continued, biting down on his bottom lip and itching to pull the trigger on both of them.

"Where's my shit?" Jarvis asked.

"Son, it's been in the backseat waiting on you while you were out adding bodies to your count and acting a fool!" Spin said. "I'm not mad. It's nothing I wouldn't have expected out of you. Just like I knew you would spare Big Shawn's life and take the others out with no remorse. We are family, Jarvis, and there's no need to feel as if we are here to play games," Spin said as he walked toward the back of the SUV, grabbed four duffel bags, and tossed them on the ground.

"It's all there. Now let me and Big Shawn be on our way. Oh . . . and next time you feel the need to pull your guns on either my men or me, be sure to leave us like the useless men you've slain tonight," Spin said fearlessly.

"Let's go, Shawn," Spin added as he helped him into the car and hopped into the driver's seat himself. "That plane offer is still on the table, son."

"I'm cool, Spin!" Jarvis retorted.

"See you around!" Spin said as he pulled out of the motel parking lot, leaving behind his three dead men.

Jarvis grabbed the four duffel bags and carried them over to his Navigator, tossing them into the backseat. He was fortunate that no one awoke through the silent corruption. He grabbed the rest of his belongings inside the motel room and made his departure, heading south on I-95.

* * *

Agents Clemons and Norton couldn't believe how quickly Jarvis had killed the three men.

"The man definitely had some mean artistry," Clemons admitted.

"Yeah, I can agree," Norton responded.

They were back on Jarvis's trail and had notified Jacksonville police of the three dead men in the motel's parking lot. They badly wanted to intervene and stop Jarvis, but the rules were cut and dried.

"If Jarvis isn't in any imminent danger, do not blow your cover," Director Bernie Scott had informed Clemons and Norton.

When they saw how quickly Jarvis had evened the odds against him and nailed the big men before they had a chance to blink, Clemons and Norton retreated and enjoyed the rest of the show.

"He's getting off an exit," Norton said.

"Gainesville, Florida. He's only fueling up . . . something that we need to do," Clemons said as she grabbed the SUV walkie-talkie and spoke to her backup.

"Delta-9, take up trail for a moment."

"Ten-four, Delta-9 cover," backup Delta-9 responded.

"Let's fuel up and then get back on him. Delta will cover for us," Clemons said to Norton, who accelerated to a nearby gas station.

Twenty - Four

Joshah maneuvered through the darkness inconspicuously while dressed in all black from head to toe. When he emerged from the wooded, rural area in Valdosta, Georgia, he saw a light illuminating the entire kitchen in the two-bedroom house. He had successfully deceived the watch team that had kept around-the-clock surveillance on him, by club hopping and disguising himself as a Jamaican man, wearing a wig of dreadlocks.

He left the club with a flow of traffic as a completely different person. The frustrated surveillance team had lost his trail, and now their jobs were in jeopardy.

There were no dogs or other animals to disturb Joshah and give him away. He had almost taken a step, until he saw the gleeful couple walk into the kitchen hugging on each other. They stood at the base of the sink, smooching.

"Perfect shot!" Joshah exclaimed as he aimed his P89 at the couple; however, he had other plans, and a quick kill would only ruin them. So he lowered his weapon and proceeded to accomplish his mission.

He approached the front door and knocked twice, startling the couple.

"Who is it? It's five o'clock in the morning!" the man called out.

It's death! Joshah wanted to say.

"Newspaper delivery," Joshah said, disguising his voice and sounding like a teenage boy.

"Newspaper? When did we start getting the newspaper, baby?" the man asked as he came to open the door.

"I don't think . . . !"

The white man answered the door and was immediately speechless as he stared at the masked man aiming a P89 at him.

Joshah didn't waste any time pulling the trigger twice and hitting the man in his chest—for too much time was enough to plan a superhero movie, and he had no time for heroes.

When the female heard the noise, she ran around the corner in her robe to investigate what sounded like gunshots.

"Dave . . . what is that?" she stopped mid-sentence when she saw the masked man standing over Dave's lifeless body.

While staring directly at the woman, Joshah pulled the trigger two more times, hitting Dave in the head. She tried to scream, but Joshah aimed at her too, and she froze.

"Why, Amy . . . ?"

Oh my God! I know that voice! Amy thought as silent tears fell from her face.

"I asked why, Amy?" Joshah said as he walked up to her and stared down at her trembling body. He took the gun and traced the front of it along her jaw line.

Amy was a beautiful redhead who he had met at a hotel in Jonesboro. The twosome hooked up a couple of times and began to form a strong level of intimacy. However, she got busted having sex with him in her Chevy Malibu in the parking lot during her lunch break.

The person who caught her happened to be her boss, and she instantly tried to fire her, until Amy screamed rape. Her boss had been a victim of rape herself and felt bad for her, and she called the police. So Amy had Joshah arrested. Now

Joshah was back to pay her a visit and deliver her a one-way ticket to hell!

He continued to trace the gun along her jaw line and then parted her robe to reveal her perky breasts.

"You miss how I used to suck on them ice cream cones, Amy? Huh?" he asked.

"Please, Joshah! Don't hurt me. I didn't plan to go forward with the case. I promise. I . . . was scared to lose my job," she said, tremulously and timorously.

"So you chose to have me arrested . . . and then you have the nerve to be shacked up with another man. I get it. Slay the black sheep, huh?" Joshah yelled as he ripped off her robe. "Give me a reason to let you live, Amy!"

"Please, Joshah! I'm sorry. I really love you . . ."

Smack!

"Awwww!"

"Bitch! You don't love me!" he exploded, after backhanding Amy to the ground. "You loved how easy it was to lie! Now die, bitch!" Joshah screamed as he pulled the trigger repeatedly.

Boom! Boom! Boom! Boom! Boom! Boom!

Joshah emptied the entire clip and then inserted a fresh one for the road.

He had a long drive to Florida, where his cousin, Vibe, was expecting him in Tallahassee. And he planned to get there with no roadblocks.

* * * * *

Barns was waiting in his office, growing impatient by the moment, waiting on the Valdosta Police Department Chief to call him back with the results of checking up on Amy Springs. When he got the news that Joshah was AWOL, he immediately thought about a rapist's profile. He knew that they would often go after their victims. He then decided to have the authorities check on Amy, if it wasn't too late.

"I can't believe them son of a bitches let him get away!" Barns exclaimed in frustration.

"Detective Barns?" the female receptionist of the Major Crimes Department called out over his desk intercom.

"Yes, Melody? Go ahead."

"You have the chief from Valdosta on line three."

"Thank you, Melody."

"Welcome, Barns," Melody retorted, using her sexiest deliverance.

Detective Barns wasted no time clicking over to take the call from Chief Arnold Smith.

"Hello, Chief . . . this is . . ."

"Son, we have a problem. I just got with your chief. He'll be calling you soon, but I need you to come out to Valdosta and break this case. Amy Springs and her lover, Dave Franzese, are both dead!" Smith informed Barns.

"Shit!" Barns exclaimed.

* * *

When C-Murder saw his target make a hurried exit in a black Yukon GMC from his place of employment, he immediately put his dark ocean-blue Ford Taurus in drive and began to trail him.

"Damn! This motherfucker's in a hurry!" C-Murder exclaimed, trying to keep the Yukon in his eyesight and not give away that he was trailing it.

The SUV then made a right turn, but broke abruptly at the descending railroad post gates. When C-Murder came around the corner, five cars behind, he saw the post gates down, which prevented all traffic from moving any further. He then heard the train.

"Saved by a train!" C-Murder exclaimed and then chuckled, for he was grateful it arrived at a good time.

"A fuckin' train would stop my ass! Great!" Detective Barns exclaimed, pounding the steering wheel.

I got to call Chythia, he thought as he grabbed his phone attached the charger.

"Chythia!" he yelled into the iPhone, which immediately dialed her number. The phone rang twice before she picked up.

"What's up, baby?" she asked her husband.

"Where are you?"

"I'm on my way to interview Shaquana Clark again at her school," she told him.

"Joshah Bennette went AWOL last night, and his victim and her lover were slain. I'm on my way . . ."

Detective Barns's attention was focused on the lengthy train, and he never saw the masked gunman approaching him from behind with an assault rifle in his hands.

"How do you know it's him, Danny?" Chythia asked.

"Baby, listen . . ."

Chop! Chop! Chop! Chop! Chop! Chop!

The AK-47 shots took Detective Barns by surprise, smashing through his tinted windows and hitting him in his chest, neck, and head. He was ambushed, and there was no way for him to escape. C-Murder opened the door and snatched the phone from his bloody hands.

"Danny! Danny . . . are you alright?" he heard a woman's voice yell out in rage.

"Danny is no longer with us," C-Murder said as he then tossed the phone back to a dead Detective Barns.

When he turned on his heels to escape, he saw an old lady talking on the phone to the police, from the panicked look on her face. She was in a purple Acura and looked to be in her sixties.

"Learn to mind your business, lady!" C-Murder said as he then pulled the trigger on her.

C-Murder hopped back into his car and made a clean getaway.

Free Daquan! he thought with elation.

* * *

Detective Chythia Barns couldn't believe her ears. She had just listened to the irrefutable, distinctive sounds of assault rifle shots. As she rushed to the location that came moments later on her radio, she swiped the inevitable tears away.

"Please, Lord, don't take him away!" she cried out.

She was only fifteen minutes away from Jonesboro, but it felt like she would never make it.

"Officer down. I repeat . . . officer down 187!" an officer announced over the radio system.

"Save him, damn it! Save him!" Detective Chythia Barns yelled. "He's not 187. He's passed out. He has a vest!"

When she made it to the scene in seven minutes sharp, she was greeted with an innumerable count of Jonesboro police.

"Detective Barns . . . please clear the way!" Chythia shouted as she forced herself through the crowd.

When she made it in sight of her husband's bullet-riddled SUV, the Chief of Jonesboro Police quickly grabbed her in an embrace, preventing her from seeing the gruesome scene of her husband's slain body.

"I can't, Chythia! I can't! He's gone. I can't let you see him like that!" Chief Derrick Jones said.

Chief Jones was a tall, muscular black man in his fifties, who had loved Detective Danny Barns like a brother.

"Nooo! Pleeeease, bring him back!" Chythia cried out.

"I'm sorry, Chythia. Lord, I'm so sorry!" Chief Jones said sympathetically while rubbing her back.

* * *

When Jarvis had finally pulled up to the Holiday Inn, he sat for a moment and outstretched his arms. He was grateful not to have been stopped by any state troopers, especially with his Georgia plates.

She said that when I get here, she'd call me, Jarvis thought.

His instincts told him to step out of the Navigator, so that's exactly what he did. As he stretched some more, his iPhone rang. He reached into his black Boss jeans and retrieved it. After seeing the unlisted number, he answered the call.

"Hello!"

"I see you're late, Jarvis. I was expecting you hours ago. Do we have any problems?" Tameka asked.

"Nah, there's no problem. I had to drive with caution. Police turned up like stop signs the entire ride," Jarvis lied.

"I can go for that. I'm glad you made it safe. Now listen . . . go into the hotel and check yourself into a room. Shower and go put on something nice. You know how I like my men. Take the money up with you, and leave it all under the bed. At twelve o'clock, your ride will be there to pick you up. And Jarvis . . .?" Tameka said.

"Yeah!" Jarvis answered.

"Please bring no toys . . . and no tricks!" Tameka suggested before she hung up.

"No toys! Ha!" Jarvis said with a chuckle.

"The last motherfuckers who said no toys got a red day. What makes you special?" Jarvis retorted as he walked inside the hotel to book a room.

Twenty - Five

Darkness had fallen when the two guests pulled up to the plush mansion in north Miami. When the back door of the limo opened, Jean was taken by surprise as he stared at the beauty of death aiming two P89 silencers at his face.

"You must be Jean," she said as she pulled both triggers twice, landing hollow points in his face.

The other Haitian men in the vicinity heard the muffled shots but thought nothing of it until Jean's body hit the pavement. Still seated in the back of the limo, she aimed at the rest of them.

"Hey . . . aye . . . aye!"

She knew there were four men, and three were in her line of fire . . . with one already down. They were all in a panic as her bullets rained on them, sending them all to their deaths.

The new rule was that whenever the boss lady showed up, no weapons were allowed around her, so none of the men were armed.

Only maids were inside the mansion, so she quickly emerged from the backseat and made a dash for the front door. When she called Jean, she disguised her voice as Tameka. He then told her to expect company, so the boss lady was sure to be mad.

Coming up the stairs, she heard distinctive sounds of a woman moaning.

What the fuck! she thought as she removed a spare key from her PZI black jeans and placed it in the knobless door.

"Pleeease stop. It hurts!" she heard the woman cry out.

"Shut up, bitch!" a familiar male voice said.

As she pushed open the door, she couldn't believe her eyes. Champagne looked at her sadly with a stream of tears rolling down her face.

The man slamming his enormous dick into her was nonchalant and unaware of his surprise visitor.

"Pleeease help me!" Champagne cried out in pain. "He's raping me!"

When the man realized she was talking to someone else and not him, he turned toward the doorway and saw two P89s pointing at him.

"Oh shit, Co—"

Before D-Zoe could finish what he was saying, he jumped off of Champagne; however, his body was hit with every bullet that came out of her gun.

Champagne jumped off the bed and ran up to her rescuer.

"Coco! How did you know? Thank you!" Champagne cried out, hugging the woman who had just killed the rapist D-Zoe.

"Let's go! We need to go now!" Coco said, grabbing Champagne by the hand and making a hasty escape. Both women got inside the limo, as their driver, Chinadoll, mashed the gas.

The rental limo and Coco's rescue plan had all come together successfully. She was saving Champagne for a lot of reasons, one of which was that she didn't deserve to die.

"We got to get you cleaned up, so we can get back to the A, because shit just ain't right down here!" Coco said.

"Thank you, Coco!"

"You're welcome . . . and you don't owe me shit!" Coco told her.

* * *

Jarvis had been fully dressed for over an hour and sitting in the same spot awaiting the final tick to twelve o'clock. He was dressed in an expensive all-black Polo suit, dress shoes, and a nice gold Rolex. He wore a bulletproof vest under his shirt and had a small .38 snub nose strapped to his ankle. Despite Tameka's warning, Jarvis refused to take any chances with his life.

He looked at his Rolex and saw that it was 11:59 p.m.

One minute, he sighed as his phone rang.

"Hello!"

"Come downstairs and walk to the back door of the limo. Leave the door cracked . . ."

"What you mean cracked?" Jarvis asked perplexed.

"Jarvis . . . leave the door cracked so that my men can get the money!" Tameka exclaimed as she hung up the phone.

"Bitch!" he yelled out. "This shit don't smell right!" Jarvis said as he did as he was told.

When he came downstairs and walked to the back door, he was greeted by a swarthy six five bodyguard who weighed at least 300 pounds. He held out his hand in front of Jarvis, indicating him to stop in his tracks.

"Turn around and let me pat you down. The boss lady wants no weapons inside . . ."

"She told me that once, big homie. I don't need to be patted down," Jarvis said, cutting the big man off.

"Look, man! Don't make my job hard. Just do what you're told," he told Jarvis, with a frown on his face.

Jarvis didn't want to cause a scene, so he quickly turned around and let the big man frisk him.

When the big man got to Jarvis's ankle and felt the .38, he tore it off with one vigorous pull.

Shit! Jarvis thought.

"Boss lady said no toys, man! You should have listened!" the big man said breathing heavy.

He then opened the back door to the limo.

"He's clean, boss lady."

"Thanks, Jeff. Let's move out now," Tameka's voice came out of the limo.

When Jarvis stepped inside, he immediately was enthralled at her scintillating beauty.

"Hello, Jarvis. Glad to see you again. Here . . . have a drink and enjoy yourself. Because we have a long night ahead of us," she said seductively, with her legs crossed and a champagne flute in her hand.

As she handed Jarvis a glass, he was skeptical at first; however, he saw they were drinking from the same bottle.

"Thanks!" he said, grabbing the glass and downing it in one big gulp. "More please!"

He held out his glass as the limo began to move. He had no clue where they were going, so he asked as she poured his drink.

"Meka . . . where are we going?"

Her iPhone rang, and she answered, but only talked briefly.

"Hello."

"It's all there, but it's counterfeit," the caller said, causing Tameka to smile.

"Thanks. I knew that it would all be there," she said as she hung up.

"I'm glad you came clean with everything, Jarvis. I guess you really do love her."

"I do, Tameka! I'm sorry that things didn't . . ."

Damn! She got me! Jarvis thought as he began to mumble and drift away. He could see Tameka laughing as she reached into her purse.

When he saw the chrome .380, he tried to move, but he was paralyzed.

Damn! he wanted to say, but he couldn't open his mouth to utter a word. *I was poisoned! The bitch poisoned me!*

"Goodnight, Jarvis," Tameka said as she pulled the trigger, hitting him in his chest. She watched him slump to the other side of the limo seat.

"Slow down and pull over!" Tameka commanded the driver while putting up her chrome .380.

The driver immediately pulled over as another limo pulled up behind them a moment later. When the back door opened, Cuban Black pulled Tameka from the car.

"Go to the car now!" he said while pulling out his .44 Bulldog.

"What's wrong?"

"Go, Tameka!" Cuban Black yelled as all hell broke loose.

FBI agents swarmed the duo, with their weapons aimed at them. Tameka instantly came out of her heels.

"FBI . . . get the fuck down now!" Agent Clemons screamed, with more than a dozen FBI unmarked SUVs and cars boxing them in.

They were on a side road next to a trailer park, and Tameka took her chance and ran. As she sprinted through the woods, a couple of agents gave chase until Cuban Black made his .44 Bulldog bark.

Boom! Boom! Boom!

The agents quickly grabbed cover and returned fire at a fleeing Cuban Black.

"Go after him!" Clemons screamed as she hopped in her unmarked and burned tires getting to the next street.

"I can't believe this bitch just ran!" Clemons yelled out in rage as she came through the trailer park neighborhood.

"Fuck!" she exclaimed when she saw all the trailers.

She could be anywhere! she thought as she then heard shots.

Boom! Boom! Boom!

Agent Clemons hopped out of her SUV with gun in hand, and followed her instincts. She ran toward the back end of where Cuban Black and Tameka had to have run, from the direction from which they took off. When she neared a back alley, she saw Agent Norton with his flashlight, searching under the trailers.

"I can't believe this shit, Norton! Them fucking limos were in our way!" Clemons said while searching the dark and praying to find Tameka Rowland, who had just become her worst enemy and fugitive.

"Agent Clemons . . . there are 160 trailers in this park and just as many across the street," Agent Donald Curry said.

"Shit! Lock this place down. Half and half search trailers . . . everything!" Clemons commanded. "K-9 back up . . . move in!" she screamed into the radio. "I can't believe the bitch took off like that!" she exclaimed in frustration.

"It's okay, we're going to get them, Clemons. Don't stress yourself," Norton said, trying to cheer up his partner.

But he knew as well as Clemons that the duo had escaped. He too didn't want to believe it.

"K-9 unit in route, ten-four!" the call came back on Clemons's radio.

* * *

The pain in Cuban Black's side and shoulder was getting the best of him. He had been shot, and he was trying his best to keep up with Tameka through the dark woods. She knew the area well, being that it was where she had grown up.

"We're almost there, baby. Hang in there!" she called to him.

"I'm trying, baby. I'm trying."

They were three blocks away from where it had all started.

He brought the FBI with him. I told him to keep the police out of it. Now he's a dead man, and she will be too when I get back to her, Tameka thought as she came to a ditch.

"Baby, we have to cross this ditch!" Tameka said.

"Where are we going, Meka?" Cuban Black said, wincing in pain.

"Home, daddy! We're going home! Back to Miami!" Tameka said as she helped her lover, friend, and partner cross the ditch.

Epilogue

Three Months Later

After continuing to be set back for trial, Daquan and Tittyboo were finally sitting at the same defense table in their expensive tailored suits while listening to Mr. Goodman give his closing argument. The trial was a shoot-out between both lawyers defending their clients, and Mr. Matthew Brooks, the black lethal prosecutor, and his backup, Catherine Evans, who was an unattractive heavyset white woman, but also with a reputable name.

"People . . . we've sat here for two weeks straight . . . day by day," Goodman addressed the twelve men and women on the jury, looking them all in their eyes.

"And the state hasn't convinced me at all that these two boys did this alleged crime of capital murder!" he retorted as he then spun on his heels to look at the audience, where he met eyes with Brenda.

Brenda was seated in the front row with Champagne, Maurice, and her niece, Shaquana. The look she gave him warmed him up and comforted him. He knew that he was doing an excellent job representing Daquan. He had no choice but to perfect his famous speech and get her nephew off the hook. Mrs. Gina Brown sat at the table with a smile on her face, loving how Mr. Goodman was handling his business.

"No gun! No DNA! No eyewitnesses, people!" he yelled, getting his point across. "Why do we have these young boys on trial?"

Prosecutor Matthew Brooks was devastated since he had lost all his pretrial motions to bring in inadmissible evidence against Daquan and Tittyboo. He was feeble and walking on eggshells by presenting a completely circumstantial evidence case, which, alone, would rarely lead to a win by the prosecution in Georgia. With hate in his eyes, Brooks watched Mr. Goodman give the jury a victory closing argument for thirty minutes. His stomach was now full of butterflies as Goodman came to an end.

Damn it! Brooks thought.

"People . . . please! Before we picked this jury, Mrs. Brown and I asked each and every one of you if y'all could use your common sense. And every one of you said yes. I ask you again to please use your common sense. Your Honor . . . defense rests!" Goodman sat as he sat down.

"State . . . do you have any rebuttal?" Judge Stuart asked the prosecutor.

Brooks stood and looked over at the defense table while pulling on his suit coat.

"No, sir, Your Honor . . . state remains rested."

The shock in the courtroom audience could be heard through silent mumbles and grunting.

Mr. Brooks knew that he'd made a mistake bigger than presenting the case after the results of his pretrial loss. But he was too deep in to pull out now, and a useless talk would only frustrate him further. Cindy's sister, Bay-Bay, and T-Zoe's family sat behind him staring daggers into his back, and he could feel their pain and disapproval as to how he presented his case against the killers of their loved ones.

"Well, then I would like to address the jury now. It's time to deliberate and come to a unanimous decision, people," Judge Stuart said as he then read off the rules and instructions for the jury to follow before he had them escorted to the deliberation room by the bailiff.

Damn! This shit is almost over! Daquan thought as he looked over at Tittyboo, who had gained more weight and seemed nervous.

"It's okay, shawty. We already home, man. Ease up!" Daquan whispered.

"Yeah, I'm cool, bra. I'm just ready, that's all!" Tittyboo whispered back.

Daquan briefly looked backed and smiled at his family and brother-in-law, who he was eager to chill with and who had been holding him down like a real nigga.

A half an hour had passed when the jury filed back in wearing their poker faces.

The foreman handed over the verdict to the sexy, white, blonde clerk of court, and she then handed it to Judge Stuart.

"Is this decision final, foreman?" the judge asked.

"Yes, sir!" the heavyset man responded.

"Okay then . . . clerk read," Judge Stuart said and sighed.

It was hard to determine if the sigh was of relief or a dead giveaway. The foreman addressed the court and spoke.

"We the jury of Jonesboro, Georgia, on counts one and two, for the murders of Cindy Mendor and Migerle Pierre, find defendants Daquan Coleman Clark and Thorton James Petway . . ."

To be continued in Two Masks, One Heart IV

BOOKS BY GOOD2GO AUTHORS

To order books, please fill out the order form below:

To order films please go to www.good2gofilms.com

Name:_____

Address:_____

City: _____ State: _____ Zip Code: _____

Phone:_____

Email:_____

Method of Payment: Check   VISA   MASTERCARD

Credit Card#:_____

Name as it appears on card: _____

Signature: _____

Item Name	Price	Qty	Amount
48 Hours to Die – Silk White	$14.99		
A Hustler's Dream - Ernest Morris	$14.99		
A Hustler's Dream 2 - Ernest Morris	$14.99		
Business Is Business – Silk White	$14.99		
Business Is Business 2 – Silk White	$14.99		
Business Is Business 3 – Silk White	$14.99		
Childhood Sweethearts – Jacob Spears	$14.99		
Childhood Sweethearts 2 – Jacob Spears	$14.99		
Childhood Sweethearts 3 - Jacob Spears	$14.99		
Childhood Sweethearts 4 - Jacob Spears	$14.99		
Flipping Numbers – Ernest Morris	$14.99		
Flipping Numbers 2 – Ernest Morris	$14.99		
He Loves Me, He Loves You Not - Mychea	$14.99		
He Loves Me, He Loves You Not 2 - Mychea	$14.99		
He Loves Me, He Loves You Not 3 - Mychea	$14.99		
He Loves Me, He Loves You Not 4 – Mychea	$14.99		
He Loves Me, He Loves You Not 5 – Mychea	$14.99		
Lost and Turned Out – Ernest Morris	$14.99		
Married To Da Streets – Silk White	$14.99		
M.E.R.C. - Make Every Rep Count Health and Fitness	$14.99		
My Besties – Asia Hill	$14.99		
My Besties 2 – Asia Hill	$14.99		
My Besties 3 – Asia Hill	$14.99		
My Besties 4 – Asia Hill	$14.99		
My Boyfriend's Wife - Mychea	$14.99		
My Boyfriend's Wife 2 – Mychea	$14.99		
Naughty Housewives – Ernest Morris	$14.99		
Naughty Housewives 2 – Ernest Morris	$14.99		
Never Be The Same – Silk White	$14.99		
Stranded – Silk White	$14.99		
Slumped – Jason Brent	$14.99		

Tears of a Hustler - Silk White	$14.99		
Tears of a Hustler 2 - Silk White	$14.99		
Tears of a Hustler 3 - Silk White	$14.99		
Tears of a Hustler 4- Silk White	$14.99		
Tears of a Hustler 5 – Silk White	$14.99		
Tears of a Hustler 6 – Silk White	$14.99		
The Panty Ripper - Reality Way	$14.99		
The Panty Ripper 3 – Reality Way	$14.99		
The Teflon Queen – Silk White	$14.99		
The Teflon Queen 2 – Silk White	$14.99		
The Teflon Queen 3 – Silk White	$14.99		
The Teflon Queen 4 – Silk White	$14.99		
The Teflon Queen 5 – Silk White	$14.99		
The Teflon Queen 6 - Silk White	$14.99		
The Vacation – Silk White	$14.99		
Tied To A Boss - J.L. Rose	$14.99		
Tied To A Boss 2 - J.L. Rose	$14.99		
Tied To A Boss 3 - J.L. Rose	$14.99		
Time Is Money - Silk White	$14.99		
Two Mask One Heart – Jacob Spears and Trayvon Jackson	$14.99		
Two Mask One Heart 2 – Jacob Spears and Trayvon Jackson	$14.99		
Two Mask One Heart 3 – Jacob Spears and Trayvon Jackson	$14.99		
Young Goonz – Reality Way	$14.99		
Young Legend – J.L. Rose	$14.99		
Subtotal:			
Tax:			
Shipping (Free) U.S. Media Mail:			
Total:			

Make Checks Payable To:
Good2Go Publishing
7311 W Glass Lane,
Laveen, AZ 85339

CPSIA information can be obtained
at www.ICGtesting.com
Printed in the USA
LVOW04s1433181116
513601LV00008B/419/P